A match made i

"I love you, Althea—you are *so* beautiful," murmured the young man into my ear.

Well, I was willing enough. I looked up at him from under my eyelashes. "I love you too," I confessed. I averted my gaze and added privately, "You are *so* rich."

Unfortunately, I apparently said this aloud, if just barely, and his hearing was sharper than one would expect, given his other attributes.

"I beg your pardon? You love me *because* I'm rich?"

"Not *only* because of that," I hastened to assure him. He also was reasonably amiable and came from a good family. He admired me and was apparently willing to overlook my lack of fortune, all points in his favor. And, yes, he was rich. Quite enough to turn the head, and capture the heart, of an impressionable and impecunious young girl such as myself.

"So . . ." He thought this over. "If I lost my money, you wouldn't love me anymore?"

"If I became ill," I countered, "so that my hair fell out in clumps and my skin was covered with scabs and I limped, would you still love me?"

"Egad!" He stared at me, evidently attempting to picture this. He turned a little green.

"But," I said, "most likely those things will not happen. You are rich and I am beautiful. We should make an excellent couple. Our children will have my looks and your money." At least, so I hoped. Only imagine a child with his lack of neck and my lack of funds!

OTHER BOOKS YOU MAY ENJOY

Keeping the Castle

PATRICE KINDL

speak
An Imprint of Penguin Group (USA) Inc.

SPEAK

Published by the Penguin Group
Penguin Group (USA) Inc.
375 Hudson Street
New York, New York 10014, U.S.A.

USA / Canada / UK / Ireland / Australia / New Zealand / India / South Africa / China
Penguin Books Ltd, Registered Offices: 80 Strand, London WC2R 0RL, England

For more information about the Penguin Group visit www.penguin.com

First published in the United States of America by Viking,
a member of Penguin Group (USA) Inc., 2012
Published by Speak, an imprint of Penguin Group (USA) Inc., 2013

THE LIBRARY OF CONGRESS HAS CATALOGED THE VIKING EDITION AS FOLLOWS:
Kindl, Patrice.
Keeping the castle / by Patrice Kindl.—1st ed.
p. cm.
Summary: In order to support her family and maintain their ancient castle in Lesser Hoo,
seventeen-year-old Althea bears the burden of finding a wealthy suitor who can
remedy their financial problems.
ISBN: 978-0-670-10438-5 (hardcover)
[1. Social classes—Fiction. 2. Courtship—Fiction. 3. Castles—Fiction.
4. England—Social life and customs—19th century—Fiction.
5. Great Britain—History—1789–1820—Fiction.]
I. Title.
PZ7.K5665Ke 2012   [Fic]—dc23   2011033185

Speak ISBN 978-0-14-242655-5

Book design by Nancy Brennan

Printed in the United States of America

1 3 5 7 9 10 8 6 4 2

ALWAYS LEARNING   PEARSON

To my writers' group, with special thanks to Karen Beil.

And to Dante, my own Fido

WITHOUT THINKING HIGHLY either of men or of matrimony, marriage had always been her object; it was the only honorable provision for well-educated young women of small fortune, and however uncertain of giving happiness, must be their pleasantest preservative from want.

—Jane Austen, *Pride and Prejudice*

Cast of Characters

➤ AT CROOKED CASTLE ➤

Miss Althea Crawley

Mrs. Winthrop, Althea's mother

Miss Prudence and Miss Charity Winthrop, Althea's stepsisters

Master Alexander Crawley, Althea's brother

Fido, a dog

Pegeen, an elderly horse

(SERVANTS AT CROOKED CASTLE)

Greengages, the butler

Cook, a cook

Annie, a maid

Jock, a groom

Tom, the kitchen boy

➤ AT GUDGEON PARK ➤

Sidney, Lord Boring

Mrs. John Westing (Fanny), his mother

Mr. Hugh Fredericks, cousin of Lord Boring

Mrs. Fredericks, his mother

{ SERVANTS AT GUDGEON PARK }

Withins, the butler

Susan, a seamstress

{ VISITORS TO GUDGEON PARK }

The Marquis of Bumbershook

Mr. Vincy, an industrialist

Mrs. Vincy, his wife

Miss Vincy, their daughter, an artist

A number of eligible young men

➣ NEIGHBORS IN AND AROUND ➢
LESSER HOO

Mr. Godalming, a gentleman suitor

Sir Quentin and Lady Throstletwist

Miss Clara Hopkins

Mr. Bold, the vicar, and Miss Sneech, his niece

Dr. and Mrs. Haxhamptonshire, the local physician and his wife

The Eliots, a large family

Leon, a small boy, and his nurse

1

WE WERE WALKING IN the castle garden. The silvery light of early spring streaked across the grass, transforming the overgrown shrubbery into a place of magic and romance. He had begged me for a few moments of privacy, to "discuss a matter of great importance." By this I assumed that he meant to make an offer of marriage.

"I love you, Althea—you are *so* beautiful," murmured the young man into my ear.

Well, I was willing enough. I looked up at him from under my eyelashes. "I love you too," I confessed. I averted my gaze and added privately, "You are *so* rich."

Unfortunately, I apparently said this aloud, if just barely, and his hearing was sharper than one would expect, given his other attributes.

"I beg your pardon? You love me *because* I'm rich?"

"Not *only* because of that," I hastened to assure him. He also was reasonably amiable and came of a good family. He admired me and was apparently willing to over-look my lack of fortune, all points in his favor. And, yes, he was rich. Quite enough to turn the head, and capture the heart, of an impressionable and impecunious young girl such as myself.

"So . . ." He thought this over. "If I lost my money, you wouldn't love me anymore?"

"If I became ill," I countered, "so that my hair fell out in clumps and my skin was covered with scabs and I limped, would you still love me?"

"Egad!" He stared at me, evidently attempting to picture this. He turned a little green.

"But," I said, "most likely those things will not happen. You are rich and I am beautiful. We should make an excellent couple. Our children will have my looks and your money." At least, so I hoped. Only imagine a child with his lack of neck and my lack of funds! The poor man's head looked exactly like a melon, or perhaps one of those large orange gourds from the Americas, bursting out of his cravat. And he had such big red lips, which he licked incessantly.

We each were lost in our own separate thoughts for a moment, I mourning the fate of these hypothetical offspring, he, as his subsequent commentary proved, considering the finer distinctions of desire and avarice.

"It's not the same thing," he said at last, looking sulky. "Admiration of a woman's beauty in a man is . . ." he waved a hand, searching for the mot juste . . . "it's spiritual. It shows that he has a soul." His gaze swept up and down my form, lingering regretfully on my bosom, which was exposed enough for interest and covered enough for decorum. He licked his lips. "But," he went on, withdrawing his gaze, "any consideration of the contents of a man's purse by a lady he is courting is—I regret to say this to one I held in such high esteem only a few short moments ago, but I must—it is mercenary and shows a cold heart. I must withdraw my protestations of ardor. Good evening to you."

He bowed, turned, and stalked out of the garden. I sighed. When would I learn to speak with a tactful tongue? There went another one. I kept forgetting how ridiculously sensitive and illogical men were. He assumed that his fortune would buy a beauty; I assumed that my beauty would procure me a rich husband. It seemed much the same thing to me, but evidently what was permissible in a man was not in a woman.

Ah well. There was yet time; I was but seventeen.

❦ ❦ ❦

"My dear, Mr. Godalming just hurried away. He was almost *rude*. You didn't say anything to upset him, did you?"

It was my mama, appearing at the entrance to the shrubbery accompanied by my small brother, Alexander.

"Yes, I am so sorry, Mama, but I am afraid Mr. Godalming has discovered that he has a soul above marriage to such a one as I. We have parted forever, I fear."

"Oh dear, and he seemed so devoted!"

"Yes, Mama, but you would not have enjoyed being patronized by *his* mama; you know you would not."

"My love, I could bear anything for your sake."

"Well then, *I* could not bear to be patronized by his mama. It is for the best. We shall do much better by and by," I said, linking my arm with hers and drawing her back inside the castle walls.

"I certainly hope so. To be honest, I do not think Mr. Godalming is a man who could make you happy," she said, putting my brother down on the frayed carpet. "So I am glad you are not to wed him. However," she admitted, "the whole east wing *does* need a new roof, or so I fear." My mama cast her eyes upwards to a tracery of green mold on the stone walls.

"Oh," she added, "and that balcony out over the guardhouse is sagging; the wooden framework is rotten."

"It would be easier to tear it down than to replace it," I suggested, and Mama agreed.

Our home was not a real castle in the sense of being ancient and fortified. My great-grandfather had been a romantic, fond of reading about the gallant knights of the Round Table, and it had been his childhood dream to build a castle by the sea. While influenced by the ruins of Castle Scarborough some miles away, he had not been a stickler for historical accuracy. Indeed, much of the structure was nonfunctional in any but a decorative sense, with winding stone stairs leading to nowhere, murder holes so improperly placed that they could pose no danger even to the most oblivious of intruders, and a hodgepodge of towers and battlements sticking out at random. He called it Crawley Castle, but such was his love for the picturesque that the building produced was immediately and invariably known as "Crooked Castle."

My great-grandfather had sold most of his holdings in order to build this fantasy on a hundred-foot cliff over-looking the North Sea, and then spent most of the rest of his fortune furnishing it. Since he had exchanged rich farmland for barren chalk cliffs, our family's financial situation has yet to recover from this architectural extravagance. Now our home, as inconvenient and eccentric as it was, made up nearly the sum total of our wealth, save for a pittance in rents, and for a time following my father's death our retaining even *that* was in doubt. His decease took place shortly before the birth of my brother, and for several months we lived in suspense. Had the child been a girl we would have had to leave our home and go, who knows where, in order to make way for the male heir, Charles Crawley, a second cousin none of us even knew, living somewhere in Sussex.

The birth of dear little Alexander saved us from that fate, and ever since his birth it has been the object of all our care to save the property for him (and incidentally for ourselves) when he shall be of an age to hold it.

Two years ago my mother remarried, to a man of fortune but no property named Winthrop. Mr. Winthrop was a widower with two daughters, both several years older than myself, and he had had great plans, enthusiastically seconded by my mother, to repair and refurbish the castle.

Neither Mr. Winthrop nor his plans survived the first month of marriage. He began to cough as he walked my mother down the aisle and did not leave off until a renowned physician, summoned from York at vast expense, closed his eyes in death two weeks later. His money descended to his daughters with only a pittance to us, and we therefore found ourselves in much the same situation as before the marriage with the exception of having two more mouths to feed. My stepsisters did feel *some* obligation to contribute towards their upkeep, but the sum was ever in dispute, and tardy in payment.

We could not afford to live in and maintain the castle; neither could we quit it. In order to lease it out to a tenant it would be necessary to make some rather expensive repairs, and even had we wished to sell it we could not: it belonged to little Alexander. Other than abandoning it to tumble into the sea, we had no other alternative but to live in it as cheaply as could be contrived and put our hopes in the future, which, sad to say, looked little brighter than did the present. We had no aged, wealthy relative teetering on the brink of eternity, and it would be many years before Alexander could make any attempt to repair our fortunes. Besides, we doted on him and did not like to think of his risking his life and health in the gold fields, or at the helm of a privateer sailing the high seas.

No, our only hope was in marriage. Mine.

I smiled upon my mama. "We shall have a new roof, the furniture new-covered, and three elegant gowns, all for you, upon the occasion of my wedding, you'll see," I assured her. "Perhaps I should consider an elderly suitor," I mused. "They are more easily managed, I believe. And *they* often have defective hearing, which might be quite an advantage."

My mother was shaking her head, but I went on, unregarding.

"Then too, you know, if I chose a man of great age and infirmity I might become a wealthy widow quite soon after the wedding. And then we could have the drawbridge over the moat replaced immediately rather than having to wait for him to recover from the wedding expenses; it has become a bit infirm of late."

"Oh, I believe it would be better not," interrupted my mama, "not until we have no other options. Best to aim for a younger man. You see, dearest, there are certain aspects of marriage—" She bent her head as she helped Alexander to climb up upon her lap—"it is not proper for you to know about them yet, but you must trust me to know what I am speaking about—that make a young man much more pleasing."

"Mama." I took her hand and pressed it, speaking earnestly. "I well understand that the pursuit and acquisition of a wealthy husband is my lot in life, and that achieving that goal is our only chance of assuring ourselves a comfortable future. I shall not disappoint you, I promise."

"Occasionally," my mama said, with a hint of defiance in her voice, "I wonder if it would not be possible for a lady to make her way in the world without a husband or inherited fortune. I feel that you and I are *nearly* as clever as most of the men we know."

"Oh, my dear madam! How you do go on!" I laughed and squeezed her hand. There were times when I felt as if I were her elder, wiser sister. Indeed, my life would have been a good deal easier in many respects if she had been a more worldly, realistic woman, but in spite of this failing, I loved her dearly. "You know quite well that it has been scientifically proven that a woman's small brain is not capable of understanding much beyond matters of the household. Tho' when I think of Mr. Godalming's brain . . . But no, intelligence is not all that counts in life, but power as well, and a woman without money has none." I gave her hand another squeeze. "I will find someone, do not fear."

She smiled then, and laughed a little. "You are right, of course, as always. I am a lucky woman to have such a daughter. Both lovely *and* practical."

"Only lucky to have a daughter like Althea? What about us, Stepmother dearest?" My stepsisters, Prudence and Charity, entered the corner of the great hall that stood duty with us for a drawing room. I sighed. I believe my mama did as well, but hers was a tiny, noiseless sigh in comparison with my gusty exhalation, which was powerful enough to flutter the lace on my bodice.

"You know I consider myself lucky to have *all* my daughters, Prudence," she said.

"Yes, I should think you might, Madam," said Charity, smiling unpleasantly. Prudence smirked.

These sneers at my mother referred to the fact that *their* incomes were essential to keeping the walls about us standing. If one or both married, the castle most likely would fall down around our ears. As things were, they were unwilling to open their purses or to authorize any purchases not for their own comfort or pleasure.

Quite providentially, my stepsisters were both disagreeable and incapable of disguising the fact. Whenever they went to call upon ladies with marriageable sons or brothers, the young men would turn pale and bolt out of doors even into a driving rain, claiming to be going out with the dogs. They knew, you see, how determined the Misses Winthrop were to marry and establish independent households. Of course, given the size of their dowries, they would no doubt succeed some day.

"I saw Godalming leaving," observed Prudence. She was the elder, with a broad, flat face and figure, and few pretensions to beauty. Her favorite pastime was collecting quotations on the subject of death and mortality. She wrote them out in an elegant hand, decorated them with sketches of weeping willows and mourning urns, bound them up in an album labeled "Memento Mori," and then gloated over them. "He seemed in a bit of a hurry. I trust you did not chase him away with that indiscreet tongue of yours, Althea."

"Indeed, I am afraid I did, Prudence. We shall see him no more."

Charity seemed much put out. "I call that selfish of you, Althea! If you didn't want him, it might have occurred to you that Pru and I . . . well, *we* enjoyed his company. He is a most eligible young man." Charity was several years younger than her sister, with a graceful figure, a great many spit curls plastered over her forehead, and a mean little face like a gooseberry.

"My apologies," I said, bending my head to hide a smile. I was quite certain that Mr. Godalming's proposal had been as slow in coming as it was only because he found it a struggle to make up his mind to marry into a family containing such as Prudence and Charity. "Perhaps you will see him at Lord Boring's ball. I promise to fade into the background so that he will not be frightened away."

Charity said, "See that you do, then. I know that Prudence is partial to him," and she cast a sly smile at her sister. Prudence preened herself.

My mama and I exchanged glances. Of the two sisters, Charity was by far the more attractive—if it were possible to ignore the sharp expression in her eyes and the pinching of her lips, one might call her pretty. She compensated for this, however, by possessing a character as acerbic as undiluted lemon juice.

My mother was all kindness, as always. "I hope you both will have a delightful ball. Indeed, I may say I hope everyone does; we need a little gaiety after the long winter."

"I am looking forward to it," I said, which was an understatement. Lord Boring's upcoming ball was likely to bring whole flocks of eligible men from London, most of whom had yet to lay eyes on any of us. In light of this fact, it was almost a blessing that I had not thrown myself away on the likes of Mr. Godalming.

On the other hand, up here in the North of England, in a small, rural neighborhood, there were few single men with either a name or an income sufficiently good to make an offer of marriage to us. Mr. Godalming had been one of those few, and I had frittered him away. I could not blame my stepsisters for being annoyed with me.

Still, Lord Boring's upcoming ball was to put all to rights; we smiled upon each other and thought of eligible men.

2

AT THIS MOMENT OUR ancient butler, Green-gages, tottered into the room to announce our neighbor Miss Hopkins. She followed hard upon his heels into the room; indeed, she burst in upon us with such lack of ceremony that my mother started up from her seat in alarm.

"How do you do, Clara? I hope all is well?"

"Oh, yes, madam! I do beg you will forgive me my haste. I am so anxious to bring you the latest news that I cannot control my emotions."

Miss Hopkins was twenty-seven years old, the same age as Prudence. Her fortune was modest, but sufficient to support her in the event that she did not marry. She was rather plain, easily excitable, and not very sensible, but on the whole good-natured, all of which made her a valuable friend and confidante to my sisters.

"Has there been some great military victory at sea, Clara?" I enquired, without supposing anything of the sort. "Is Napoleon defeated, or the king dying?"

Miss Hopkins gave a small shriek and seized upon my last suggestion. "The king dying? No, indeed! Why should he be? No, my news is of much greater import than *that*! It is that Lord Boring has arrived at home, just in time for the ball, and he has brought a large group of gentleman friends!"

"Really, Clara!" murmured my mother, sending a reproachful glance in my direction. "Our dear monarch's health is a matter of much greater import than a neighbor's arrival at his home, with or without friends."

"Oh, of course I did not mean that that would not be a most dreadful calamity. It is only that . . . it seems so excessively *odd* that Miss Crawley would suggest that the king should die. I hardly thought it likely."

I cast my eyes to the heavens. The king had been ailing for years now, so much so that his son had been named regent, to rule in his place.

"'Let us sit upon the ground,'" suggested Prudence, pleased to be able to produce an appropriate quotation, "'And tell sad stories of the death of kings; / How some have been deposed, some slain in war, / Some—'"

"And of course, I knew you would be interested in the advent of such a large group of gentlemen into the neighborhood." Luckily, Clara thought nothing of cutting Prudence's recital short; had she not, we all would still have been sitting there when poor King Richard was carried out in his coffin in Act Five and the curtain fell.

"We *are* interested," I admitted.

"Yes, dear Clara, do tell us who is coming," begged Charity.

"Why, he has brought his friend Major Dunthorpe, and the Hadleigh twins of Cornwall, and the Marquis of Bumbershook. Five young men counting His Lordship!"

"How delightful," said my mother, and, once Clara had been guided to the safest chair (much of our furniture was apt to collapse without warning), we settled down to an amicable discussion of the young men's fortunes, manners, and characters. True, Charity once expressed her pique at Clara's comment that I would be the "reigning beauty of the ball," by a mean little pinch disguised as a sisterly pat on my arm, and Prudence twice talked over my mother's remarks and thrice flatly contradicted her, but as our little chats went, it was tolerably pleasant.

In their place, to be honest, I would find it irritating to have a much younger stepsister forever thrown up to me as the beauty of the family. However, since they each possessed a good dowry, while I had nothing but a pretty face to offer a husband, beyond an ancient name, one hundred a year, and a tumbledown pretend castle belonging to my four-year-old brother, I did not pity them overly much. And while pinches and barbed comments aimed at myself might be pardoned, I found it difficult to forgive rudeness towards my gentle mama.

Greengages brought in tea. (I had made the cakes myself, tho' this was a carefully kept secret—we could not afford a pastry chef or even a cook with a passing acquaintance with the art.) The tea itself was rather insipid, as it was our household habit to dry and reuse the leaves for a fortnight before replenishing them, and the liquid inevitably lost color and flavor. However, it was steaming hot, which was the great thing on a chilly April day like the present one, so we were quite snug. If the fire was perhaps a bit small to warm us, it was no matter; the thought of Lord Boring's upcoming festivities provided animation and cheer.

Prudence, Charity, and Clara were deep in conference over not their own dresses for the ball, as this subject had long since been canvassed, but rather the probable attire of every other young lady of the neighborhood, when Greengages reentered the room.

"Sir Quentin and Lady Throstletwist," he quavered, and cast an apprehensive look at the tea tray, no doubt wondering how long the cakes would hold out at this rate. The knight and his lady, frequent visitors to our home, looked around the room in search of the seating least likely to tip over or poke them in awkward portions of their anatomy.

"Believe this one will hold your weight, m'dear," said Sir Quentin, gallantly offering his wife the best of the available chairs.

"No, my love, you take that one. Think of your lumbago. I shall be quite comfortable here." And she sank down onto a rather rickety specimen at my left elbow. We paused, holding our collective breath as the chair creaked, swayed, and then steadied.

Satisfied that all was secure for the moment, my mother offered tea and cake to Lady Throstletwist.

"Demmed cold in here," complained Sir Quentin, chafing his hands together.

"Quentin!" scolded his wife.

"Oh, do bring your chair up closer to the fire," urged my mother.

"What fire?" he demanded, peering into the cavernous fireplace, which was so large it had in fact been used in days gone by to roast whole oxen. He squinted at the small blaze far at the back of the firebox. "Hmm, hmm, I see. Yes, I suppose there is one in there." He held his hands out hopefully towards it.

"Now, Quentin, I *told* you to dress warmly. *I* always

do when we visit Crooked Castle, even in August. You know how the winds go rushing up and down these halls, whatever the season. One might as well be living in a perpetual cyclone," said Lady Throstletwist, complacently stroking her cashmere shawl down around her plump form. She and her husband owned Yellering Hall, a cheerful modern house with a great many fireplaces, all blasting out prodigious amounts of heat. "Why your grandfather chose to build this place in such an exposed situation, hanging out over a cliff on the North Sea," she said to my mother, "I will never know. You haven't even an ocean view from inside this great, dark barn."

"Some tea will warm you, Sir Quentin," Mother said, handing him a cup.

"Thank you, m'dear," said Sir Quentin, looking with sad eyes down into the cup of pale brown water.

"One lump or two?" she asked, her hand hovering over the lid of the elaborate silver sugar caddy. I awaited his answer with some trepidation.

Sir Quentin brightened. "Oh, is there sugar? I'll have—"

"None." Lady Throstletwist finished his sentence. "Sir Quentin is watching his waistline."

This was manifestly untrue. Sir Quentin was as slender as a blade of wheat. It was simply that Lady

Throstletwist had guessed that, handsome as the caddy was, it in fact contained no sugar lumps. I had used the sugar for the cakes, which had been meant to last the week but which were swiftly disappearing. I smiled at Lady Throstletwist gratefully; now Mama need not know the empty state of the sugar caddy.

"Very wise," said my mama. "I daresay you shall out-live us all, Sir Quentin."

"Have you heard about the arrival of Lord Boring's party?" Lady Throstletwist enquired, changing the sub-ject. "Quite an excitement for us here in quiet little Lesser Hoo."

"I believe five young men are coming to enliven our neighborhood," said Miss Clara.

"I must differ with you, my dear Miss Clara," said Lady Throstletwist. "I have it on excellent authority that there will be six!"

"Miss Sneech and Mr. Bold," announced Greengages gloomily, showing yet two more neighbors, our vicar and his niece, into the room.

"How delightful," said my mama. "Greengages, more tea and cakes please." Greengages looked at her reproach-fully, but took the tray and went to boil more water in the kitchen. After seeing our new visitors seated, I took the opportunity to excuse myself and followed him.

"Oh, miss," wailed the cook when I showed myself in this domestic office. "Whatever shall we give them to eat? Your lovely little cakes are gone."

"Is there any bread?" I asked.

Cook allowed as how there was a bit of bread, "But I was planning on it for breakfast."

"Never mind breakfast. Slice it very, very thin and toast it—carefully, mind, don't burn it—then spread it with butter."

"Nay, there's none, miss," said Cook dolefully.

"Plain will have to do, then," I said. "Boil a vast amount of water," I instructed, and returned to the drawing room.

Little Miss Sneech, always anxious to think the best of everyone, credited the Baron with bringing an even larger party. "Eight young men, I hear," she was saying as I sat down next to her. She clutched my wrist with a small, hot hand. "Is it not the most *amazing* news?"

"Doctor and Mrs. Haxhamptonshire," sighed Green-gages (correctly pronouncing this, by the by, as "Doctor and Mrs. Hamster"), "Mr. Eliot, Mrs. Eliot, Miss Eliot, Miss Cynthia Eliot, Master Samuel Eliot, Miss Agatha Eliot, and Master Augustus Eliot."

I returned to the kitchen as this large group filed in.

"Tiddlers from the moat," I ordered. "Set the kitchen boy to catching them." Our moat was more of a lake than a moat. It did not entirely encircle the castle, situated as it was on the very edge of a cliff—it had been constructed solely to provide the need for a drawbridge—but it was nevertheless a sizeable body of water, regularly flooding after a heavy rain. Once upon a time it had been stocked with fish for the table, but we had eaten our way through these larger specimens long ago. Tiddlers were all that were left.

Cook looked at me doubtfully. "There's no' much eating on one of them tiddlers, miss. Wouldn't even call 'em tiddlers, I wouldn't. More like a minnow than a proper fish."

"That is why he must catch a great many of them. Have him use a fine-mesh net. Broil them and salt them and put them on one of the good platters. And then we can garnish the platter with watercress, also from the moat. I suppose we have watercress?"

"Oh, aye, miss. Any amount. Oh, and miss? The fireplace crane is rusted near through. Hope the whole great pot don't come crashing down, if you understand me. That would be a picture, that would."

"Very well. You must have Jock call in the blacksmith to repair it," I said, then called over my shoulder as I left, "Boil more water!"

As I entered the room, now choked with broken-down

and ruinous pieces of furniture dragged in from other chambers to seat the throng, I heard the cry: "Twelve of them! Actually twelve people in Lord Boring's party! We shall be quite overset!"

So long as we did not have to feed and water them, I thought, taking my place amidst the crowd, I shouldn't mind if there were a hundred.

At last, having supped on Crooked Castle's version of a Barmecide feast (and if your governess has neglected your education to such an extent that you are unfamiliar with *One Thousand and One Arabian Nights*, why then, shame on her—go and read it), the knight and his lady wife rose to take their leave. The moment Lady Throstletwist stood up, her chair shuddered and then slowly collapsed into a sad little splintered heap on the floor. Being extremely well bred, she sailed on out through the door without a backwards glance at this small disaster. Everyone else present also contrived to ignore the situation, save the younger Eliots, who giggled. On this note the party broke up, and having settled to everyone's satisfaction that the number of Lord Boring's party lay somewhere between five and fifteen, the neighbors betook themselves to the comforts of their own homes.

I assisted Greengages with collecting the soiled crockery and setting the room to rights, dragging the surviving chairs back to their proper positions.

"Tell Cook that the broiled minnows . . . er, tiddlers, were a great success," I said. "As she will see for herself, they are entirely eaten." The platters were stripped; even the watercress had been devoured.

"I will so inform her, Miss Althea," Greengages said, and staggered off with the tea tray.

Relieved that it had not been necessary to sacrifice our own dinner, a rabbit snared by the groundskeeper, to the entertainment of our guests, I was able to look forward to a peaceful evening after a turbulent day. Therefore, putting my shoulder into the task, I wheeled my embroidery out into the center of the room; then, lighting a candle, I seated myself and began to work.

It is customary for young ladies to paint a fan or embroider a purse; these elegant arts show off wifely skills and a pair of dainty hands to good effect. While my stepsisters were generally involved in this sort of project, I was unable to waste my time on such pleasing trifles. Instead, I was mending the tapestries from the great hall; a monumental task, but a necessary one, as they helped to soften and absorb the icy winds that howled through the castle in January and February.

Besides, without them, the great hall of Crooked Castle bore more resemblance to one of His Majesty's less attractive prisons than to the home of a family of an ancient and honorable name.

The current tapestry I was repairing was as large as the dimensions of the room in which I worked. In order to render it more manageable, it had been fan-folded and stacked in great piles on its own wheeled table. On pleasant days, with the aid of Greengages, the groundskeeper, and the kitchen boy, I had the whole conveyed out into the sunlight so that my stitchery would run true. On evenings like this I used a cheap tallow candle and hoped.

I was soon joined by my stepsisters and mother, who were chattering quite cheerfully together after the success of our impromptu entertainment. Prudence even complimented me on the refreshments in her patchy and inaccurate French.

"*Les très bons hors d'oeuvres, mon enfant*," she said, edging her chair in front of my mother's next to the fire, thereby casting Mama into cold and darkness. "A delightful, crisp texture!" she continued in English, baffled by the French for *crisp* and *texture*. "But I could not determine what, precisely, I was eating."

"Thank you, Prudence," I said, without enlightening her. Prudence cherished delicate sensibilities when it came to her diet, and undoubtedly the crisp texture was due to the fact that the little creatures were made up almost exclusively of skin and bones. One day I feared I should have to direct Cook to fry up some species of insect, as I am informed is done in some of the wild places of the world, in order to feed my family. Should that day ever arrive, I almost hoped Prudence would uncover my deception and fall into a swooning fit, but no—the ensuing screams would destroy any pleasure thus gained.

As we were not yet arrived at that extremity, we ate our simple repast (a ragoût of rabbit, each lady being further refreshed by a thimbleful of wine poured into a cup of water). My mother went up to kiss Alexander goodnight and then we listened to Charity reading from *The Mysteries of Udolfo* (a most enthralling tale) whilst we sewed, with no further news or excitements save Miss Clara's stable boy, sent to tell us by way of an addendum, that Lord Boring's sister had now been confirmed to have accompanied her brother.

Exhausted by this further good fortune (for an amiable sister to such an eligible man is a great advantage to young ladies, who can call upon her from morning till night in hopes of catching sight of her brother), we retired to our chambers rejoicing.

3

LORD BORING AND HIS mother, the Honorable Mrs. John Westing, had but lately moved into the district. We had of course been acquainted with old Lord Boring, the present Lord Boring's uncle, who, having suffered from ill health nearly all his life, he had excused himself from much visiting amongst the neighbors, so we had never been intimate. Our relationship was almost entirely limited to our asking, "How do you do, my lord?" and being told, "I am sorry to say that I do poorly, very poorly indeed." After many years of this—my entire lifetime, in fact—he apparently did even more poorly than usual, and died.

The new young lord (known until his elevation to the peerage as Mr. Sidney Westing) had remained in Town upon succeeding to the title, sending his widowed mother ahead to put the property to rights and to make herself known to the district, with the assurance that he would follow her as soon as he completed his course of study at

Oxford. We had called upon her and she had returned those calls, tho' she'd seemed in no particular hurry to do so. Our position in the neighborhood and our ancient, if not noble, family name demanded both respect and courtesy, but apparently the smallness of my mother's income meant that Mrs. Westing's civility rose to a certain level and no further.

She had, however, repeated to us the promise she had made to every young lady in the neighborhood of a ball to be held at Gudgeon Park "when once I have gathered my wits together and learned my way about the place." Four months had evidently been sufficient time to refurnish the house and to understand the ins and outs of so small a community as Lesser Hoo, and so the promised ball was about to become a reality.

Balls were not a common experience for us; Gudgeon Park was by far the largest estate in the place and the former Lord Boring's health had not permitted (or perhaps had exempted him from) these sorts of entertainments. Beyond Crooked Castle, Yellering Hall, and Gudgeon Park, there were no large houses, or even inns of sufficient respectability and elegance, in which to host a dance of any size. Our neighbors the Throstletwists considered themselves too elderly to make the effort, while the Eliots, whose finances might stretch to a simple jig or gavotte after supper, could not conceivably manage a cotillion. And of course *our* limited income did not allow us either to give balls ourselves or to travel to Bath or London, or even York, where such festivities were commonplace.

From Lesser Hoo to Hasty, and from Little Snoring to Hoo-Upon-Hill, nearly everyone under the age of ninety was looking forward to the event. The farmers and trades people were pleased by the steady stream of orders for geese and pigs, candles, slippers and hair ribbons in the weeks before the party, and the entire district was stimulated and interested by the new faces glimpsed on the streets, in the shops, and riding over the moors. The older members of the gentry anticipated a good gossip, a game of cards, and a fine meal in a house most had not visited in a decade or more. But it was the young ladies and gentlemen who were most affected; we were half mad with excitement and anticipation. We longed to be dancing.

At last the night of the ball was upon us. My stepsisters arrayed themselves in costly new gowns sent up from London, their modest store of jewelry, and towering feather headdresses for which whole colonies of egrets must have given up their lives. Their complexions came out of a bottle labeled "Bloom of Ninon de L'Enclos."

This popular cosmetic is almost entirely composed of white lead, or so our apothecary tells me, and I cannot help but think it may prove unwholesome. Passing by Penelope's room I saw them each taking it in turn to apply great handfuls to the other's face and neck, occasionally coming over dizzy as they breathed in the fumes, and then lying down on the bed to recover. I expressed my concern, suggesting that moderation might be the best course, and was roundly snubbed and ejected from the room.

My mother and I were by necessity attired much more simply, in old dresses mended and new-trimmed. The repairs had required great ingenuity on my part. Added ornamentation, so useful in covering flaws, was forbidden by the simplicity of the styles now fashionable. My mama could employ her shawl to hide a bad burn on the back of her best muslin, and then sit on it for most of the evening, but I, who would dance before the view of the company, was at my wits' end as to how to mend several tears in the hem of my best dress.

The rips were caused by Charity's rather too rapidly following me up a flight of stairs. This came about as a result of her claiming that, as she was my elder, I must allow her to go first. I protested that the rules of precedence were not meant to be so strictly observed in casual encounters between family members, especially while ascending the pokey back staircase next to the butler's pantry when I had my small brother in my arms. I therefore went on ahead of her. The ensuing scuffle had resulted in the rents I now needed to disguise.

This episode, incidentally, had left its mark on my spirit; ever afterward I found myself unable to mount a staircase without thinking of Mr. Coleridge's immortal words:

> Like one, that on a lonesome road
> Doth walk in fear and dread,
> And having once turned round walks on,
> And turns no more his head;
> Because he knows a frightful fiend
> Doth close behind him tread.

I know I ought to be more charitable towards my stepsisters, but it is quite beyond my power.

In the end I gathered the hem every few inches to create a scalloped effect. Since the dress was no more than a slender white wisp of gauze with cap sleeves and a low neckline, this modification seemed to me charming rather than ornate, and the mended tears quite vanished in the pleats thus formed. Any family jewels had long since been sold, and so with some fresh flowers from the garden and a satin ribbon to tie back my curls, my toilet was complete.

When once little Alexander had been put to bed—he wept at our going and we had to promise to bring home a handful of sweetmeats from the ball before he consented to stay with Annie, Mama's maid—it was time to leave.

Our carriage was a battered old chaise, and rather small to convey four passengers. We were obliged to sit nearly on top of one another, a fact that my stepsisters felt to be so injurious to their dignity that they insisted on stopping to alight a good way from the front entrance of Gudgeon Park, so that they would not be observed scrambling out of such a crowded and humble vehicle. I was doubtful about the weather, fearing we should find ourselves wetted through before reaching shelter, and said as much. However, my mother was anxious to please her stepdaughters and overrode my protests. She climbed out and I followed. Prudence and Charity, finding themselves much more comfortably circumstanced now we were got down, decided to remain in the carriage and be conveyed right up to the door rather than walking the rest of the way.

"You do not mind, Stepmama? I am sure you do not, for you are all goodness," said Charity.

"Oh, pray go ahead and do not regard us," said my saintly mother, while I fumed by her side. "It is no more than a step or two to the house, and it would be a shame to crush your lovely gowns any further."

"Mama!" I cried as the chaise rolled away. "Those ill-bred, ungrateful—"

"Hush," she said. "It does not signify at all, my dear. We are but a few yards from the door—"

"But those rain clouds!"

"And I flatter myself that we have timed our arrival to a nicety. The storm will hold off until—"

C-r-rack! Boom!

The heavens opened and rain poured down upon us. Mama clasped my hand and we ran for the great stone staircase fronting the house. We could not wait for the footman to escort us with his sheltering umbrella, but burst unceremoniously through the doorway. We found ourselves under the critical gaze of Mrs. Westing and her butler, who were greeting guests in the front hall.

"How excessively *wet* you are," remarked Mrs. Westing, regarding us through a lorgnette. "Withins, fetch something for the ladies to dry themselves with."

"How kind," said my mother. "As you can see, and hear—" the thunder boomed out again, "the tempest is upon us."

Withins did not bestir himself, but snapped his fingers at a maid, who went to fetch us some dry cloths.

"How good it was of you to invite us!" continued my mother, attempting to salvage the situation. "And how wonderful to see a ball at Gudgeon Park again!"

When at length we were dismissed from Mrs. Westing's presence by the arrival of the maid, we paused a moment to tidy ourselves, blotting the moisture adhering to our gowns and our persons and rearranging our hair. The great gilded mirrors in the hall assured us that, while still somewhat damp, we looked perfectly respectable. Indeed, as we made our formal entrance into the ballroom our eyes were bright and our color high. I smiled on my pretty mama, thinking that she might be my sister, so young did she look.

How glorious it all was! I had not been in the house for years, but my recollection was of a great deal of dust, old-fashioned furniture, and gloomy dark landscapes lining the walls. Now all was light gleaming on polished wood, rich fabrics, fine silver, and exquisite French wallpapers, which, given the embargo, must have been smuggled in. Spiky and inedible-looking pineapples, the first I had ever seen, formed the centerpiece of the main table in the dining room. I smelled flowers and heard the sound of laughter and low music.

Prudence and Charity had not waited for us, but had made their entrance unencumbered by their poor relations. As we moved to join them I could not help but cry, "Oh, delightful!" A handsome older woman seated nearby smiled and nodded at me and said, "It is, little *sirène*" (meaning mermaid, you know, and referring to my damp state).

Annoyed at this attention being paid to me by a distinguished-looking stranger, Prudence ordered in an undertone, "Hush. Do not speak until you are spoken to."

"Remember you are the youngest, Althea," said Charity, "and must not thrust yourself forward."

"Oh, certainly," I said composedly, my temper restored by the sight of the glittering scene before us. "What a handsome man," I added.

"Be silent!" said Charity. "Where?"

"*Will* you hold your tongue, Althea? Everyone will hear," whispered Prudence. "Oh, I see who you mean. He has a fine countenance, has he not?"

"He is coming this way."

Indeed, a number of young men were coming this

way from all corners of the room. I knew I was thought a beauty by Lesser Hoo standards, but I had not been certain that gentlemen accustomed to the great ladies of London and Bath would agree. Evidently, they did.

I once saw a demonstration of what happens when a large and powerful magnet is introduced into the presence of a great many iron filings. This situation rather reminded me of that: heads turned, bodies realigned, gentlemen stood up, excused themselves and began to drift slowly but inexorably in our direction. Some in the crowd, of course, were old acquaintances, but they also drifted towards our corner, except for Mr. Godalming, who pointedly turned his back on me. Alas, poor Mr. Godalming. Perhaps I *had* been rather rude to him, tho' inadvertently. However, I soon lost sight of him in the throngs converging upon us.

Prudence and Charity closed ranks. They stood in front of me, blocking me from the view of the assembly and smiled on the young men queuing up for an introduction to our family. As Prudence pressed me back against the wall she made contact with my dress. "Ugh!" she protested. "You are quite horridly damp!" Still she pushed me ever further back until I feared a trampling. Taking one of my damp ringlets in my hand, I shook it vigorously so that a few droplets of cold rain water flew out and landed on the nape of her neck. She gasped and moved forward, and I breathed again.

The identity of the handsome young man reached our corner before he did; he had to arrange an introduction from Sir Quentin before speaking to us, while Gossip stands on no ceremony but leaps o'er all boundaries and will not be checked by rules of proper behavior. He was in fact our host, Lord Boring.

The knowledge that he owned this imposing house and extensive property could only enhance his fine face and figure, which were further flattered by his faultless evening dress: his neck cloth was of dazzling white lawn starched to a fare-thee-well and tied with mathematical precision, and an exquisitely well-cut long-tailed coat revealed a muscular yet slender build. Indeed, so overpowered were my stepsisters by the combination of masculine beauty and great wealth that they clutched at one another for support and fanned themselves energetically as they were introduced. Or perhaps it was the aftereffects of the Bloom of Ninon de L'Enclos.

"Mrs. Winthrop, Miss Winthrop, Miss Charity Winthrop." The Baron bowed his acknowledgments to each lady. Sir Quentin, having performed his duty in pronouncing our names (save mine, for I was invisible in my corner) had walked off in obedience to a command from his wife.

"And this is . . . ?" The Baron bowed again, craning his neck to peer at me around the veritable thicket of egret feathers which decorated my stepsisters' hair.

I could not see Prudence's and Charity's faces, as their backs were towards me, but I could judge the thoughts flitting through their heads by the long silence that ensued. My mother was not attending to our conversation—her notice had been claimed by the lady who had called me a mermaid and who was now making her acquaintance. My stepsisters were therefore debating the possibility of disowning me, perhaps, in view of the simplicity of my attire, identifying me as a passing maidservant. However, common sense won out at last and Prudence said, "My apologies, M'lord. This is our young relative, Miss Crawley." She leaned towards him and confided in a whisper, "*Poor Althea! It is dreadful of us, but we do tend to forget about her.*"

Then she went on in a loud, carefully enunciated voice, as if I was half-witted, or the age of my brother Alexander, "Althea, dear, this is Lord Boring. Our host this evening, you know. Say hello politely."

I did as she bade me and dropped a curtsey. "My lord," I said.

Lord Boring lifted what I could not help but feel was a satirical eyebrow at my stepsisters. *"Enchanté,"* he said to me, bowing. "I am delighted to make your acquaintance, Miss Crawley. I believe your father was Mr. Thaddeus Crawley of Crawley Castle. I am sorry never to have met him, but my uncle spoke highly of his kindness and courtesy as a neighbor." He turned to Prudence, while keeping an eye on me, and said, "Ladies may find a younger female relative forgettable, but no gentleman would agree that a young lady such as Miss Crawley ought to be overlooked for so much as a moment."

Prudence replied, still in a whisper, *"Oh! She's pretty enough, but . . ."* She tapped her lips twice with her fan, nodded in an exaggerated fashion, and gave him a look of deep significance. Uncertain of whether I was being represented as simpleminded, demented, or merely dowerless, I contented myself with a smile and the observation that, while Gudgeon Park had always been a noble estate, his mother's efforts in the past few months had transformed it into a veritable enchanted palace.

My stepsisters burst into derisive laughter. "Really, Althea!" said Charity. "An 'enchanted palace'! What a phrase!" And she in turn leaned forward and whispered, *"Such a naïf! A mind like a child's. The poor thing!"*

"In fact," said Lord Boring, "I quite agree with Miss

Crawley. Those are almost the exact words I used myself to my mother not more than an hour ago."

My eyes traveled over the brightly lighted scene. I was accustomed to spending my evenings in a state of near total darkness only slightly relieved by the light of one cheap tallow dip. But here the night had almost been entirely banished by rank upon rank of beeswax candles; I could see everything as tho' we stood under a noonday sun. "Yes," I said, remembering the former state of the house, with dust and dead leaves and little clots of dog hair from the former Lord Boring's Irish setters drifting down the hallways and settling on the stairs and behind doors, "it is so much cleaner than it used to be, for one thing."

Shrieks from both my stepsisters alerted me to the fact that they regarded my words as ill-advised.

"Thoughtless, heedless Althea! We are so sorry, Lord Boring. Our deepest apologies, but you see how she is!" they cried in a confusion of voices. And, "Of course, the former Lord Boring was never very well, was he? Quite *naturally* he—And a single man, without a wife to see to the servants!"

Belatedly I realized that they were in the right. Would I never learn to tame my tongue and keep imprudent thoughts within my heart? I sighed. There went yet another young man, within moments of meeting him, and this one was far and away more desirable than Mr. Godalming, with his receding chin and his forward mama.

Lord Boring laughed. "Quite right, Miss Crawley. It *is* much cleaner than it used to be. Well do I remember it on the occasions I came to Gudgeon Park to see my uncle. My dressing room always smelled odd, for instance," he said reminiscently, "and I could never quite identify the odor. I shall pass your words of commendation on to my mother and her staff."

My stepsisters shrieked again and begged him to do no such thing.

"I shall make a point of it," he said, and put an end to their horrified protestations by engaging all three of us, in order of age and precedence, to dance, after which he bowed and moved off to fulfill his duties to his other guests.

4

". . . ALTHEA? ARE YOU THERE?" Mama was attempting to introduce me to the lady with whom she had been conversing. "Prudence, Charity, would you be kind enough to step aside so that—ah! There you are, my dear! Your stepsisters are so tall, and their headdresses are so . . . imposing, that for a moment you quite vanished behind them."

My stepsisters moved away with an ill grace. The lady, it proved, was a Mrs. Colin Fredericks, late of London, now come to live among us.

Miss Clara Hopkins leaned forward and said something to Prudence, who in turn whispered loudly in Charity's ear, *"A merchant's widow, or so Clara tells me!"* Charity's eyes grew round and she shied like a nervous filly in a thunderstorm.

Quite frankly, I too was surprised to see someone whose income derived from vulgar commerce here at the Boring ball. I knew nothing of His Lordship save that he cut an elegant figure in evening attire, but even my slight acquaintance with his mother made me believe she was unlikely to harbor egalitarian impulses; on the contrary, she struck me as a woman who, having married into the nobility from a wealthy but undistinguished family, was determined to turn her back on her own less exalted origins. I thought she would be acutely alive to the finer distinctions of rank and consequence.

"And she is, of course, the present Lord Boring's aunt and the sister-in-law of Mrs. John Westing," added Mama, thereby making all plain.

I regarded Mrs. Fredericks with interest and sympathy. It was an old tale from before I was born: a sister of the former Lord Boring, apparently bewitched by a handsome face and form, had bestowed her hand in marriage on a man in a position much inferior to hers and had, in Lesser Hoo, at least, never been seen or heard from again.

"Ah!" My stepsisters also had made the mental connection and recollected the existence of this almost mythical creature, who had been so willful in her affections as to abandon a Baron's seat in order to live above a shop in London's Cheapside.

Prudence had called Mrs. Fredericks's husband a "merchant," but I suspected that the word was a piece of embroidery on some very plain cloth. We had always been told that Mr. Fredericks was a man of no fortune or property; he was not even the proprietor of the small business where he labored for a living, but a mere hireling. And now, it seemed, he was dead, and she had returned to her childhood home.

"Oh, I *see!*" said Prudence, wagging her feathered head vigorously and making it clear to all present that the relationship alone explained the otherwise inexplicable, namely, Mrs. Fredericks's appearance at this august gathering. Still, by birth Mrs. Fredericks *was* the daughter of a baron, so Prudence and Charity curtsied, rather stiffly, and then began slowly to edge away. Only a short time ago her neat figure and graceful bearing had raised such admiration in their hearts that they had resented any attentions she might pay me. Now, as tho' fearing that such unwisdom in matrimonial matters might, like an inflammation of the lungs, prove infectious through standing near her too long, they were only too pleased to leave the three of us in peace to improve our acquaintance.

"Mrs. Fredericks was telling me that Mrs. Westing has invited her to come and live here at Gudgeon Park," explained my mother.

"We are both widows now, you see," said Mrs. Fredericks, "and she has kindly offered me a home. Then too, there is a great deal to be done to Gudgeon. My brother had not the health or spirits to oversee the estate. I believe I can be of real assistance to Fanny—my sister-in-law, you know—and to my nephew."

"I am sure you can," I said. Her clever, sensible countenance and ready smile suggested that Mrs. Westing had reason to congratulate herself on procuring both a companion and a domestic drudge of a high order, with no need for wages or an afternoon off. "How delightful that we are to have another new neighbor at Gudgeon Park," I said, with perfect sincerity, for my mother appeared quite pleased with her company and she would be a pleasant addition to our circle of friends. A long immersion in the world of commerce did not appear to have coarsened Mrs. Fredericks's taste or weakened her intellect, and the two ladies soon were launched on a knowledgeable and detailed discussion of the latest in poetry and literature.

I left them to it, having no leisure to join in; Sir Quentin was approaching with a long string of young men craving an introduction. As I began a series of curtsies so numerous as to make me quite giddy, I had only a moment to reflect that the simple elegance of Mrs. Fredericks's toilette was no doubt due to her sister-in-law's anxiety that she not shame her in public. She wore no jewels, and that pretty gown was no doubt a hand-me-down. Mrs. Fredericks's early training and natural good taste had done the rest.

The first dance was to begin, and I could spare no more attention for Mrs. Westing's sister-in-law, however pleasant. Several of the gentlemen had managed to avoid being introduced to my stepsisters and were therefore able to ask me to dance immediately instead of having to work their way through my relatives first, so I was quite well occupied. I danced first with my most exalted admirer, the Marquis of Bumbershook. He was not the "young man" we had been promised (Lord Boring's sister also proved to be apocryphal, and his party numbered only the original five Miss Clara had suggested), being fully five-and-forty, but nevertheless an agile and accomplished dancer and a person of some wit and great kindliness. During the moments when our attention was not required for the execution of the dance, we conversed, and I soon found myself speaking to him with the ease and comfort of long acquaintance.

"And so here I am," he said, "come to join my young friend Boring in his new home, thinking that it would be a generous act to support him in his sad removal from the gaieties and fine society of London to the duties and dullness of the countryside, far from civilization up here in the North of England. And what do I find? A handsome house, a fine property and"—bowing—"new neighbors so superior to anything I could have expected—some of them indeed positively sparkling with intelligence, elegance and beauty."

"Fie, sir," I said. "I fear that 'sparkling' is not a term one may, with propriety, apply to my dear friends and neighbors." Here my eyes strayed to Sir Quentin, who was engaged in loudly blowing his nose on an enormous handkerchief, quite as large as a small tablecloth, and his lady, who was equally loudly scolding him for his bad manners. The Marquis noted where my gaze had fallen and smiled, but without a hint of malice. "We are a quiet, homely set of people, my lord," I chided him, "and we do not deserve to be made fun of, even by a marquis."

"I should not dream of doing such a thing," he protested. "Perhaps my eyes were dazzled by present company, but in truth I do believe that the society to be had in your village and outlying areas is most agreeable, and the countryside hereabouts is attractive, as well. Boring is far more to be envied than pitied."

I raised my eyebrows. "Indeed, my lord, you are in the right *there*. I shall save my pity for a more deserving object than a handsome young man who has joined the ranks of the aristocracy and inherited a great fortune in the process."

"Oh well, as to *that* . . ." the Marquis began, but then thought better of it, and fell silent. Immediately afterwards we found ourselves swept back into the dance.

After the Marquis I danced with Majors Dunthorpe and Simpson, and then once more with Lord Boring.

I must confess I was delighted with Lord Boring. His dancing was not as good as the Marquis's but to tell the truth, the Marquis was so good as to make my own efforts seem slow and stumbling in comparison, at least in my own eyes. Lord Boring moved gracefully and well, but without the fire and brilliance of his guest, for which I was thankful.

I enquired how he was enjoying his new home.

"Very well indeed," he replied. "I am fond of Town in the season, but once the hot weather sets in, who would not rather be in the countryside? Now that I have left Oxford, I have every expectation of becoming a thoroughgoing countryman and making the best of my rustication."

I smiled, acknowledging his jest—"rustication" was more often used in the sense of having been expelled from college, of being exiled to the country rather than going to live there of one's own choosing.

"I hope you will not find our company a punishment," I said. "Your new neighbors are pleased to have a larger, and perhaps more lively, household than your late uncle's established here at Gudgeon Park. We hope to please and entertain you enough to keep you here for much of the year. I believe your mother is fond of whist and hazard and other games of chance. I fear she will find few partners here, at least not for high stakes. We do not gamble more than sixpence at a time in these parts."

Lord Boring agreed that his mother was a great card-player, but confessed he himself was but an indifferent one. He preferred to be out of doors, he said.

"Are you a keen horseman?" I enquired.

"I am, and I look forward to exploring the neighborhood. The cliff walks along the sea appear to be very fine, as are the great stretches of moorland I see about me—my horse and I are anxious for a good gallop."

"You are city-bred, my lord?" I enquired. When he agreed, I suggested that perhaps he should have a groom show him the best places for his gallops. "For your tenant farmers will not thank you for trampling their crops, or for leaving gates open. And some parts of the moor can be dangerous, not to mention the cliff paths. Fog is always a concern on those narrow tracks above the sea."

"I can see I shall require a guide—my new life has rules and consequences I cannot guess at. But no groom could advise me as well as you—will you not put your local knowledge at my service? It would be a great kindness to a new, and ignorant, neighbor."

I smiled and said I would do all I could, and then the dance claimed our attention.

At last I returned to my mother's side—she was alone, as Mrs. Fredericks had been obliged to go and see to some arrangements in the kitchen—and she demanded an account of my time.

"I saw you standing up with the Marquis. It was an honor that he secured you as a partner so quickly," she said, "tho' of course *that* is no great cause for amazement, you being by far the prettiest girl here." Having heard my demurral and my favorable opinion of the Marquis, she then enquired about my other partners.

"Why, then it was Major Dunthorpe, and after that his friend Major Simpson, then Lord Boring, and then both the Hadleigh twins—one after another, of course—and then a Mr. Pultney, and after that—"

"You shall tell me about each of them by and by, but I am anxious to know if you have danced with Mrs. Fredericks's son. He is here, she tells me, and is excessively handsome, agreeable, and clever and just the sort of young man you would like."

"No, I don't believe we have met." The only man with whom I had danced who struck me as excessively handsome, agreeable, and clever was Lord Boring, and my eyes wandered for a moment, seeking him in the crowded room. Recollecting myself, I returned my attention to my mother and continued, "Certainly none of my partners so far has been named Fredericks."

"I am sorry to hear it. She was so sure you would like him."

I smiled. Mrs. Fredericks had seemed like a sensible woman, but she could not help being prejudiced here, and she did not know *me* at all. And whether I liked her son or no, my business was matrimony, and that to a man of means. The son of a shop assistant did not seem like a good prospect, however agreeable he might be.

On the other hand, in my judgment I had toiled long enough in the marriage market for one evening. I was quite willing to be entertained by a handsome face, a ready wit, and a pleasing manner. Seeing Mrs. Fredericks approaching with a young man by her side, I prepared to be as pleasing, in turn, as I could.

I curtsied and raised a smiling face to gaze upon a countenance so peevish and ill-tempered that my welcoming smile faltered and I stepped backwards a pace in consternation.

He was an amazingly unattractive man. Or perhaps, I decided upon brief reflection, he was not really so, when judged by his face and figure alone. These were quite good, tho' his complexion was sallow and unhealthy looking. No, it was the black scowl he bestowed on my mother and me that ruined his looks and rendered him repellent. Furthermore, he was not attired in evening dress, but rather wore a patterned waistcoat, a wrinkled neckcloth, and an old blue tailcoat liberally spattered with ink, as though he were in the habit of wiping a pen on it. The only acceptable item in this disgraceful costume was a handsome pair of Hessian boots.

I have never seen a true fop or dandy—they are London-bred birds, I fancy—and I do not think I would admire one if I did. I would not care for a man who thought more of his own beauty than of mine. But to appear in a ballroom dressed as a shabby little clerk!

As I was studying this displeasing specimen, his mother addressed him in affectionate tones, giving further proof to the adage that a mother's love is blind. "My dear," she said, "Mrs. Winthrop and her daughters live in that most remarkable structure, Crawley Castle. You know we have spoken of it often."

"Oh, yes—perfect gargoyle of a building. Foolish place to put it, out on a cliff like that," was his amiable response. "I shouldn't be surprised if the place didn't break off and fall into the sea someday."

I felt my cheeks grow hot with outrage.

"I am delighted to meet you both," he went on, looking anything but. "However, I must bid you good-bye on the heels of bidding you hello, Mrs. Winthrop, and Miss uh . . . hrmm," he glanced in my direction. "So sorry, Mother, but I told you I could not stay. Do forgive me." He bowed and made as if to leave, then turned back to say, "By the way, Mrs. Winthrop, I should get that drawbridge of yours seen to. Even a cursory inspection from the road makes it obvious that the mechanism is quite rusted through." As an apparent afterthought he added, "Good night, and do enjoy the rest of your evening," as if he were our host. He sketched a slight bow and walked away.

"Oh dear, he is *so* devoted to business," said his mama, smiling after him. "I fear that the reason you did not meet him before was because he was cooped up in the library doing sums all the evening. I had so hoped he would dance with you, Miss Crawley. I was counting on you to distract him from his everlasting accounts for a few moments at least."

"I regret I was unable to be of service, Mrs. Fredericks," I said in as pleasant a voice as I could manage, "Perhaps we will meet again."

Not if I see him coming first, I thought.

5

I AM NOT ACCUSTOMED to dancing all night. When finally we had made our grateful *adieux*, squashed ourselves into the chaise, and, wending our way down a dark and damp lane, at last discovered ourselves to be at home again, the clock was striking four and faint glimmerings of dawn could be discerned in the eastern sky. We disentangled our weary limbs, climbed down, and went yawning to bed.

We were up betimes, however, as I wished to call on the Throstletwists early enough in the day to forestall them, and our other friends, from calling on *us*. As delightful as it is to entertain one's neighbors, I prefer not to do so *too* often—the incidental expenses are rather higher than our domestic economy can withstand.

I had some difficulty in wresting Charity and Prudence from the depths of slumber, however. They wailed and attempted to retreat under the bedclothes again. When I persisted, they demanded tea and toast before they would consider rising from their beds. At last, however, with the assistance of their maid, I succeeded in getting them dressed for the day and prodded and pushed them out the front door. Collecting my mother and little Alexander, we prepared to walk to Yellering Hall.

Alas, my exertions were futile. No sooner had we gained the front walk than Charity demanded that we wait while she fetched a parasol for the sun. Once she'd rejoined us we had to retrieve Alexander out of a large bush into which he had chased a cat, and then Prudence turned back, requiring a ribbon for her hair of a slightly different hue than the one I had selected. I urged the rest of our party to press on without her, but to no avail. A large mass of humanity and horseflesh was visible, advancing up the drive. Four coaches and several men on horseback were hastening towards Crooked Castle, bent on receiving hospitality. I sighed and retreated, outmaneuvered.

However, I had resources at my command that had not been available the last time we received guests; they would not go away hungry. The strawberries were fast ripening, and there would be some cream left from the milking. It was a pity—I had planned to make strawberry jam for the winter—but there was no help for it. I murmured in my mother's ear, retreated to the kitchen and gave my directions to Cook.

I was pleased but not surprised to find that Lord Boring had come, and surprised but not pleased that he had brought along his unpleasant cousin. I had rather supposed Mr. Fredericks's presence last night to be accidental, as a result of his bumbling into the ballroom in mistake for some much humbler clerical office. Yet here he was, looking discontentedly about himself and remarking more than once that Boring had browbeaten him into making the visit; he couldn't in the least imagine why.

"Upon my word, Fredericks," exclaimed Lord Boring, "looking at these charming and lovely ladies"—he bowed to my mother and then to my stepsisters, who tittered, and finally to me—"you wonder *why* I should wish to call on them? I do believe you've lost every trace of gallantry and civilized behavior in your time away from England."

Mr. Fredericks contented himself with uttering a short, satirical laugh in response. My small brother, Alexander, looked up at him in wonder and then burst into tears, climbing into my mother's lap for comfort. Mr. Fredericks seemed somewhat nonplused by this outburst and, casting about himself for a peace offering, held out a strawberry still warm from the sun to the child. Knowing, as I did, that Alexander was stuffed brimful with purloined sweets from the ball, I did not expect this to be a success, but after a long, grave look and a hiccupping sigh, Alexander took the strawberry and began to nibble at it.

"In any case," continued Lord Boring, ignoring this small contretemps, "you know that the doctor has ordered rest and a change of scene for you, and you also know quite well that you have been itching to get a good look at Crawley Castle. As have I," he added.

"Yes," admitted Mr. Fredericks, "I have, but you rousted me out just when I was getting down to the heart of that Beddoes contract. There's something rotten there, I can smell it."

"You shall sniff out rotten contracts to your heart's content when we return. Just now we are paying a social call." His Lordship turned to me. "The Marquis, by-the-by, sends his compliments and apologies for not calling on you. He has business to attend to in York today. But perhaps, Miss Crawley, as great-granddaughter of the original owner, you would be so good as to give Fredericks and me a brief tour of the public rooms?" He bowed to my stepsisters and continued, "I should be sorry to put the Misses Winthrop to the trouble."

Prudence gave way easily enough. The Baron's appearance, wealth and position put him beyond her ambitions, though if Mr. Fredericks had only maintained his own house she might have considered him with some interest. It was harder to persuade Charity, who had some claims to beauty along with an impressive fortune, that *she* should not serve as guide. However, her friend Miss Hopkins, having already seen the attractions of Crooked Castle, such as they were, begged her to remain. And as a number of other unattached young men remained in the room she evidently concluded that without me present she could hope to work her wiles upon them uninterrupted.

As I rose to conduct them around, I reflected that Lord Boring, in common with Mr. Fredericks's mother, treated that difficult young man with an amused indulgence. This was understandable in Mrs. Fredericks, who, as his mother, was more or less required to love him, but less so in Lord Boring, who was not. Perhaps Lord Boring found Mr. Fredericks's rudeness amusing, as medieval kings were said to be entertained by the coarse and impertinent behavior of their jesters.

"Are you and your cousin intimately acquainted, Lord Boring?" I enquired. We stood a little apart from Mr. Fredericks as he paused to examine the least moth-eaten of the tapestries. "Did you grow up together?"

"No, not entirely, though from time to time he would come to stay with us, of course."

From what I knew of the former Lord Boring's attitude, there was no "of course" about it. It cast a surprisingly good light on the Westings—I should not have expected them to find the son of a shop clerk an acceptable playmate for the heir to a barony.

"Perhaps," I hazarded a guess, "he saved your life?"

A quick smile came and went across Lord Boring's face.

"Almost—but no, not exactly," he said. "I am very fond of him. And of course, we are associated in our overseas interests—he looks out for my investments in India and so on." He lowered his voice. "I owe him a great deal, more than he will allow me to say. He's a good fellow, Hugh is, tho' not very polished, I know," he said, as we watched Mr. Fredericks poking a finger through a moth hole, thereby enlarging it.

I understood, or supposed I did. Lord Boring had employed this socially inept backdoor cousin and now felt responsible for him. Presumably Mr. Fredericks was a faithful steward of his master's affairs, and Lord Boring was no doubt relieved to be able to fulfill a family obligation as well as to safeguard his own interests.

"Oh undoubtedly," I said. The "good fellow" had just

detached at least two feet of fringe off the bottom of the tapestry while attempting to tug it into place. My eyes narrowed. Someday I might have to sell those tapestries so that we could eat.

"That wants sewing back on," said Mr. Fredericks, handing the strip of material to me. "What's behind this door?"

"A passageway to the servants' quarters and the kitchen offices," I replied, but he opened it nonetheless. Unwilling to inflict this person on our long-suffering cook, no doubt enjoying a well-earned rest after whipping up all that cream, I suggested, "Perhaps you would like to follow me up to the minstrel gallery. We have a great many family portraits and other paintings, some of which are said to be quite fine." In fact, most of the paintings left were portraits, as landscapes and still lifes are easier to sell than ancestors.

The walls of Crooked Castle are pierced, more or less at random, with arrow slits. In a real fortress these small openings, just large enough to accommodate an arrow angled towards the ground, would have allowed archers inside to take potshots at an enemy outside without providing a target themselves. In an unreal fortress like Crooked Castle, their only function is to allow the winds from off the North Sea free access to the interior.

One such breeze rolled down the stairs to meet us as we mounted. Mr. Fredericks hugged himself and shivered. "You ought to have Rumford fireplaces installed—it's like an icehouse in here," he said.

"Oh, that's only because you're so used to the tropics, you know," said His Lordship, smiling bravely at me as the gust of air lifted the hair on his forehead. "Fredericks has been ill," he confided, as the gentleman in question moved ahead of us to examine the portraits. "He came back from India a few weeks ago and on the voyage home he acquired a chill on the liver that he's finding difficult to shake."

"I see." I spoke over my shoulder to His Lordship as I hastened after our other guest, who was scratching with his fingernail at the gold leaf on the frame of my grandfather's image. I'd have thought that even a chill on the liver would be pleased to be excused from Mr. Fredericks's company, but apparently not.

When I reached him, Mr. Fredericks was looking down at a small object in the palm of his hand. He held out a curlicue of gold, broken off from the frame, saying accusingly, "Shoddy workmanship. However," he went on, pointing at a painting I had loved from infancy, a small picture of a brown and black dog playing with a ball, "*that* is by George Stubbs. Take care of it. It may be worth something someday. Or not, of course—Stubbs turned them out by the boatload, you know—but it is a pleasant little thing. The others, of course . . ." He shrugged.

With enormous restraint, I did not remark that, up until today, the paintings had not suffered any damage in *my* lifetime. "Allow me to show you the view from the parapet," I said, in hopes of distracting him. What harm could he do on the battlements, out in the open air?

"These portraits ought to be cleaned," he said, ignoring my suggestion and fiddling with the painting of the little dog. "They are shockingly dirty. Let me show you . . . I believe that a penknife inserted here under the frame would allow us to see—"

"Mr. Fredericks!" I cried. "Please! I am exceptionally fond of that picture." I looked to Lord Boring for assistance, but he was some distance away, examining a portrait of my great-great-great-aunt on my father's side. He turned, however, and was about to remonstrate, when Mr. Fredericks began groping in his pocket for a knife.

"Oh, never fear, *I* shan't harm it," said that gentleman.

I gasped and, struck by inspiration, clutched at my throat. "I—I require some air or I shall faint! I must ascend to the roof. I pray you, gentlemen, follow me at once!" And I pulled the picture from Mr. Fredericks's grasp, set it down, and staggered towards the stair to the rooftop walkway.

Mr. Fredericks looked rather startled, but followed me meekly enough, once Lord Boring gave him a push in the proper direction. Once out on the parapet, with its splendid view of the sea, however, it occurred to me that the drop from where we stood to the beach below was prodigious. I eyed him nervously and moved a safe distance away. The danger, however, was not to my person but to my family's property; he began prodding at the massive stone making up the battlement in front of him, trying to see if he could pry it from its position. ("This one's loose," was his comment.)

"Fredericks, stop that at once," said Lord Boring. "You've done enough damage for one day." And he pulled his cousin bodily back from the edge.

"*I? I* have done damage?"

"You have. And if you knock that stone over you'll be held criminally liable for doing to death a whole family of fisher folk."

Indeed, peering over the edge I could see our tenants, John Snyder and his sons, dragging their boat and nets onto the beach far below us. I gasped at their peril.

"Gentlemen, indeed I pray you! Shall we not go

downstairs? And—and—" I wracked my brain for some activity which would engross Mr. Fredericks's energies without resulting in murder or mayhem.

"And we shall take our leave," finished Lord Boring. "We have trespassed on your kindness for far too long." As we moved towards the staircase he addressed me privately. "My apologies. I shall ensure that reparations are made for any harm our visit has caused."

Mr. Fredericks was still looking out to sea. "Yes, do let's go down. I was examining the cliff face that supports this portion of the castle earlier, and it is my opinion that a good storm could fatally weaken it. That moat was a foolish idea of your great-grandfather's—it undercuts the integrity of the ground this building stands on. The only thing that prevents the waters of the moat from breaking through are two thin stone walls, and a major flood could breach them. All this"—he gestured about us—"is quite apt to fall into the sea at any time."

Most thankfully we arrived downstairs without further mishap, Mr. Fredericks complaining fretfully that he had not been shown over the whole of the property. "I have not inspected the dungeons yet, Sidney, and you know how I wished to."

Lord Boring darted a swift look at my face and, smiling, said, "Another time, Hugh. I fear that today Miss

Crawley might show us in and then forget to let us out again."

To my surprise, Mr. Fredericks apologized for any alarm he may have caused—"I am enthusiastic, you see," he explained—and then he sought out my little brother, solemnly shaking hands in farewell. "I am sorry I made you cry," he said. Alexander rewarded him with a large smile and skipped alongside him in a friendly fashion all the way out to the drawbridge, prattling happily and begging his new friend to visit us again as soon and as often as possible.

I myself could not help but wonder if entertaining Lord Boring would mean entertaining Mr. Fredericks as well. As delightful as I found His Lordship, *that* would be a rather heavy price to pay for his company.

❧   ❧   ❧

The next morning a stone mason appeared at our gate, saying he had been instructed to secure the stone that so nearly had crashed down upon our tenants' heads, with the compliments of our new neighbors. Greengages questioned him and then brought him along to me.

"I—I beg leave to send my thanks to Lord Boring," I said, amazed but grateful.

"Yes, miss," he said. "Where am I to begin?"

After I had set him to work, a young woman with a basket was shown in. Greengages explained that this was Susan, an expert seamstress employed by Mrs. Westing, who had been dispatched to mend our tapestry.

"Oh, and miss?" added Susan. "This basket here is for you."

I took the basket from her, puzzled. Inside lay one of Lord Boring's cards atop a quantity of fine woolen fabric. It said, "Hoping this will make some restitution." Folding back the cloth I found that I was looking into two enormous brown eyes. "It—it's a dog!" I said stupidly.

"Yes, miss," agreed Susan. "A puppy. Two months old today."

I sank down into a chair. What on earth was I to do with a puppy? Yet another mouth to feed!

"My—my thanks to His Lordship," I said.

The tiny black and brown creature—a perfect copy of the dog in the Stubbs painting—had no doubts as to what I should do with him. He climbed out of his nest in the basket and began the arduous journey up to my lap, pawing and scrabbling with his fat little legs. He looked up at me, reproachful at my lack of response, and for a moment I thought I glimpsed a will of steel in those sweet, rather bulbous brown eyes. Obediently, I helped him up and, with a loud sigh, he curled into a ball and fell asleep.

Evidently I now had a dog.

Greengages reappeared, breathing hard from this unusual exercise. "*This* person says he's come to clean and repair the pictures," he said.

"Well then, I suppose you had better show him to the picture gallery, hadn't you?"

Perhaps, I decided, entertaining Mr. Fredericks was not without its benefits, if His Lordship always felt the need to make good the damages caused by his friend.

6

THE AMOUNT OF FINANCIAL assistance ladies can properly receive from a gentleman unrelated to them is limited. During the week following the first visit by Lord Boring and his cousin, workers swarmed over the castle: the drawbridge was repaired, the battlement stonework secured, the tapestries mended (save the largest and most dilapidated, which I was mending myself), and the paintings cleaned. This was delightful, but the expense on Lord Boring's part could barely be justified as reparations for the damage Mr. Fredericks had caused. The drawbridge, for instance, had not been harmed, but it was indeed broken and since so much other work was being done, we allowed the repair to be made. But when the stone mason proposed rebuilding the fireplace in the small sitting room to a more efficient, modern design we felt it necessary to refuse, however regretfully.

Lord Boring and Mr. Fredericks called again, on their

own this time, as most of their other visitors had departed. In obedience to a sharp look from His Lordship, Mr. Fredericks remained in his seat and broke nothing save a toy of Alexander's, a small model of a horse and cart. However, as he spent the rest of the visit repairing it, pulling wire, pins, and other oddments from his pockets and modifying the fixed wheels so that they rotated like those on a real cart, and adding reins and a real horsehair mane and tail, we could not complain. Indeed, Alexander brought him all his other toys, in hopes that he would break them too.

"You must allow us to express our indebtedness for the repairs made to the castle," I said in a low voice to Lord Boring, bending over my embroidery so as to avoid his eyes, "which have encompassed far more than was injured by Mr. Fredericks." I halted, wishing that I possessed a tactful tongue. I *could* have expressed thanks without mentioning Mr. Fredericks—I did not want to sound as if I were reproaching Lord Boring for his friend's loutish behavior.

"I pray you, speak no more of it to *me*. I did nothing of any importance," said Lord Boring, looking rather self-conscious. We both glanced out of the corners of our eyes at Mr. Fredericks, who was running the little cart back and forth on the carpet, testing out the new wheels and entirely oblivious to our embarrassment on his behalf. As His Lordship seemed not to want further thanks, I changed the subject.

"The dog," I ventured, looking down at the animal in my lap, "is affectionate. Remarkably so, in fact."

Indeed, the dog had proved to be faithful almost to a fault. He had taken up the attitude that he should accompany me at all times, even on the most private of occasions. When I sat, he was on my lap. When I walked, he was at my heels. If I made any effort to exclude him, he behaved as if I had struck him. His small face became a picture of woe: his soft lips wobbled and his enormous brown eyes bulged tragically at me.

While my stepsisters shared a bed (mostly to keep warm—there were eighteen bedrooms in the castle, some even furnished with beds, so there was no need to share from lack of accommodation), I had been accustomed to sleeping alone since childhood. The dog refused to allow this arrangement to continue: the moment I lay down he would commence pawing at the side of the bed and whining, demanding to be lifted up to join me. Once his desire was achieved he would stretch out, managing (tho' very small in his person) to take up most of the available space.

Sometimes while I slept he was stricken by an overwhelming compulsion to express his devotion, an urge frustrated by the fact that nearly all of my anatomy was submerged in bedclothes. He would therefore drape himself over my head and sigh into my ear, causing me to dream of being engulfed by an infatuated fur-lined hat. Most mornings I found that I had been cuddled and cosseted right up to the edge of the bed and was on the brink of falling off.

In addition, he snored.

However, as irksome as this may have been, I will confess that on those few occasions when I awoke and did not feel his little body pressed up next to mine, I sat bolt upright feeling quite offended until I had located him on the bed.

At my words Mr. Fredericks looked up from his repairs to my brother's toy. "Oh, do you like him? He's from an excellent stud. He ought to be a fine animal when he is grown."

This being by far the most amiable remark Mr. Fredericks had ever addressed to me, I took care to respond graciously. Apparently he had assisted Lord Boring in the procurement and choice of the puppy—to judge by his behavior one might think he alone was responsible—and when I asked a few questions about proper feeding and handling, he proved well equipped to answer them.

"And what is the puppy's name?" enquired Lord Boring.

I blushed. I'd thought of calling him "Sidney," but feared this would be too presuming. And should Lord Boring and I ever find ourselves on intimate enough terms to address one another by our first names it would be quite confusing, as well.

"'Dog' is what I mostly call him," I admitted.

The assembled company began to propose names. Prudence and Charity favored such suggestions as Trouble and Nuisance. I will confess that he *did* leave a puddle in their room, but as I myself cleaned it up as soon as it was discovered I did not see why they should so dislike him.

"Call him 'Fido'—meaning faithful, you know—since he is so attached to you," said Mr. Fredericks in the tone of voice which ends a discussion. "And now, Boring, we must go. Or I must, at any rate. *You* may wish to waste the entire rest of the afternoon, but *I've* business to attend to. Good-bye, Fido," he said to the dog, which wagged its tail in reply.

"But—Lord Boring!" I said. "I have not yet heard *your* suggestion for the dog's name."

"Oh, I expect Fredericks is right and you ought to call the little fellow Fido."

Upon hearing the word *Fido*, the traitorous dog wagged its tail again.

"There, you see?" said Mr. Fredericks, a sudden smile lighting up his narrow face.

My mother added, "Fido is a lovely name. Good dog, Fido," and the dog wriggled all over in a paroxysm of delight.

I sighed. Evidently the dog had a name. And it was a name chosen by Mr. Fredericks, rather than by the man who had given him to me.

"Good-bye, Master Alexander," said Mr. Fredericks, presenting the much improved toy to the boy. "See that you take care of that mare and her equipage," he admonished, "and don't haul in too hard on those reins or she'll bolt on you. Miss Hrrm," he said to me, "that thread you are using is poor quality; it will break under stress, and if it does not, it will rot in these damp, salty conditions." He turned to his friend. "Boring, I'll see about the horses." Whereupon he got up and left the room without a word to his hostess, or to anyone else.

Lord Boring made his farewells properly, like a gentleman. When they had gone, I could not help but cry out, "Why, oh *why* does His Lordship suffer the company of that *odious* man?"

Prudence bridled. "I do not find him so," she said. "Mr. Fredericks is a fine-looking man."

I raised my eyebrows in disbelief. Prudence was building hopes of attracting him as a suitor, after all. Tho' only the son of a shop clerk, he was the grandson of a baron, and that atoned for a great deal. I suppose she felt that the money she would bring to the marriage would be matched by the whiff of nobility, and the right to visit Gudgeon Park on familiar terms. How she would bring herself to forgive Mr. Fredericks's mother for her rash *mésalliance* I did not know. In any case, as he had not so much as glanced in her direction, I did not think much of her chances.

"When he smiles, he is *very* attractive," agreed my mother. "It was good-natured of him to mend Alexander's toy."

"He broke it," I observed.

"Ah, but not one in a hundred men would have spent the greater part of an hour, and the whole of their visit, on such a fiddling little job with a small child's toy. Now, if he were trying to win the esteem of the child's sister, perhaps yes, but . . ." She trailed off, eyeing me doubtfully. Even my mama, partial as she was, could not convince herself that Mr. Fredericks was in love with me, or indeed had noticed my existence, other than as the new owner of a puppy in which he had interested himself. "Truly, Althea," she went on, "I do not think his heart is bad, only his manner."

"His manner is quite enough to condemn him in my eyes," I said. "How he could *speak* of wasting the rest of the afternoon in our company! And to leave without a proper good-bye to you, Mama! I find him quite insufferable."

"You would change your mind soon enough if you believed him a man of property," said Prudence. "If he were a rich man, you'd be only too happy to set your cap at him."

"I do not deny," I said after a moment's reflection, "that I consider it my duty to marry a man of substance to ensure that little Alexander shall inherit this property in due course, and, furthermore, to ensure that my mother *and even my stepsisters* will always have a home to call their own in the event that they do not marry. But I find that I *do* have standards, below which I am unwilling to sink. I swear to you that nothing, *nothing!* could tempt me to marry Mr. Fredericks, even had he all the wealth of the Indies in his pocket."

And I swept out of the room, the dog Fido trotting close behind.

"How pleasant it is," said the Marquis of Bumbershook, "to recline at one's ease in a castle garden in June, while nearby four lovely ladies sit and sew a fine seam."

Having completed his business in York, the Marquis had returned and ridden over from Gudgeon Park one afternoon to sit with us as we sewed in the central bailey, which is open to the sky and possesses the remains of a rose garden now coming into bloom.

Prudence and Charity were far too overawed by his eminence to say much to him, leaving us in a blissful silence wherein rational discourse was possible. Rather to my surprise, my mother was uncharacteristically silent as well, tho' His Lordship was as affable and approachable as our good neighbor Sir Quentin. The Marquis and I therefore bore the burden of keeping the talk flowing, but this was no hardship. He seemed to be enjoying the pale sunlight and the brave roses that had, against all odds, struggled out of the thin, chalky soil and flaunted themselves against the stones of the bailey keep.

He had brought a small, cowhide-covered ball for the dog Fido. After some initial suspicion, Fido had grasped the purpose of this item and they began a game of toss and fetch. That is, His Lordship tossed, and Fido restored the ball to him after much racing about and hysterical barking.

I later learned that it was a "golf" ball, stitched and stuffed with feathers for the game of the same name, at which the Marquis was an adept. Had I known how expensive the ball was, I should never have allowed Fido to sink his little teeth into it. However, by the time I did learn the ball's value, it was too late. He became addicted to the diversion and expected a game of ball every night after dinner for at least half an hour. However, I digress.

Since His Lordship the Marquis was lately come from London, I pressed him for details about the new fashions, books, and plays of the capital. When he spoke of new publications my mother at last lifted her eyes from her work and began to join in. Soon they were engaged in conversation and I was pleased to note, and to observe my mother note, how his every word and expression marked him out as a man of intelligence and cultivation. One would expect polished manners and an extensive knowledge of the world from a man in his position in life, but he was better than that: he was possessed of a superior mind and a liberal nature.

I will not attempt to disguise the fact that I found

Lord Boring to be an attractive man, not only in his purse but in his person. But it would not do to be too hasty; here was yet another man who was more than worthy of my consideration.

True, he was a widower more than twenty-five years my senior, and a head shorter than I. But I believed him to admire me, and I liked him very much. No, the concern was that he was far, far too grand for me; mine was an ancient and honorable lineage, but the Marquis was a celebrated member of the *ton,* on terms of easy familiarity with the Prince Regent's residence at Carlton House and with the most distinguished houses of Europe. If he did remarry (and thousands of young ladies and their mamas must have exerted themselves to the utmost to achieve this goal, but had in the end been forced to admit defeat), it would be expected that he would choose a woman from one of the great families of England, not an impoverished young girl from the back of beyond in a dilapidated castle by the edge of the North Sea.

How foolish I was to even *think* of him as anything but a pleasant acquaintance!

And yet . . .

And yet I will admit to another side of the story. He was the last of his line—his wife and young child had died some years ago and he had no close relatives to resent his choice. He was free to marry as he pleased. Therefore, perhaps it was not *entirely* foolish, I thought as I watched him smiling contentedly around at our little family party.

Ah well, I told myself, it was early days yet.

Life in little Lesser Hoo had become much more interesting of late.

7

RAIN, RAIN, RAIN, AND yet more rain. On the day after we sat in the sunlit garden with the Marquis, black clouds rolled in off the sea bringing a driving downpour. It rained and blew and then rained some more, for five nights and days. No one came to call. The plans that the Baron and I had made to organize a riding party had perforce to be put off until the weather improved. The ladies of Crooked Castle sat indoors for days in near darkness as wind and water beat against the castle walls, and Fido and Alexander chafed at their involuntary imprisonment. One morning when we awoke we found a small stream of water trickling down the hallway in the eastern wing where Mama and I slept.

We looked at each other and sighed. There could now be no doubt that there was a hole in the roof. I had spoken to the stone mason, and he had told me that a good slate roof such as ours could last for a long time. The damp spots I showed him might be due to a few missing slates, the repair of which would take an hour or two, no more. On the other hand, the entire framework beneath the slates might be rotten, calling for a time-consuming and, above all, *expensive* undertaking to replace it. In any case, we could not afford even the least costly repair.

"Do not fret yourself, Mama," I said. "I will see to it."

"But the money—"

"I will see to it."

"Prudence and Charity would never—"

I smiled, and Mama fell silent.

We knew better than to *ask* Prudence and Charity to contribute any money towards the upkeep of this, their only home, though they could readily have afforded it. (I knew this for a fact, as I had taken care to read their last financial statement from London.) We had attempted to shame them into it before, with dismal results. A common saying in our part of the world is, "Eat all, drink all, and pay nowt"—in other words, we are not known for foolish generosity—and my stepsisters are true daughters of Yorkshire. Their position was that they were certain to marry some day, and it would be wrong to deny their future husbands and children even the smallest portion of the fortunes that had been left to them.

"Perhaps we may be blessed with large families, Stepmama," Charity explained. "Then only think how we would regret squandering money that might have made provision for younger sons, or for daughters without the means or desire to marry. No, I am sorry, but it is not to be thought of."

However, Mama knew that I had contrived to get money out of them before for some important repair or to augment our meager food budget. She did not always approve of the means I used, but had to admit that it was only fair that they pay some small part of their maintenance. Of course, every time I managed to squeeze a few coins out of them, we paid for it by having to listen to endless remarks about how lucky my mother was to have such open-handed, free-spending stepdaughters in her household.

I would be glad enough to agree with such sentiments if it meant that the roof over our heads would remain whole.

Their bedroom was on the leeward side of the castle, away from the wind and rain blowing in off the sea, which meant it was dry and secure and they were not affected by the leaky roof. It was necessary to arrange matters so that they *would* be affected, or they would never stir themselves in the matter.

It took me some hours searching in the least-inhabited rooms of the castle, as well as in several outbuildings where grain and foodstuffs were stored, to find what I required. I had to lock Fido into the pantry, and I feared that his howls and scratching at the woodwork would give away my plan, but it did not; my stepsisters were making a great noise on the old pianoforte and did not hear. Gently transporting my finds on cushions or old burlap sacks, I made several trips to the bedrooms in the same wing of the building where Prudence and Charity slept, with special attention to their chamber. Once I was satisfied with the west wing, I made certain arrangements to a bedroom on the eastern side.

Then I sat back and awaited developments.

At nightfall we retired to our several rooms and soon darkness and silence reigned over the castle. I lay awake with my door open, listening. I did not have long to wait. Shriek upon shriek split the night. I arose, pulled on a robe and lit my candle. Fido leapt to the floor and accompanied me. My mother, much perturbed by the disturbance, cried out to me as I passed her room, "Oh Althea, what dreadful thing can have happened?"

"I do not know. Remain in your room and I will ascertain what the trouble is. I do believe . . . why, yes, I believe the cries came from the west wing, where Prudence and Charity are."

Not content to wait to hear what was causing the

uproar, which was increasing in volume every moment that passed, my mother insisted on following me down the hall. As we came closer and the screams grew louder and more strident, the servants began to appear in the hallways, rubbing their eyes and yawning. I noted with interest that Greengages's nightshirt was of a virulent green color, patterned with pink flowers. Could it have belonged to his deceased wife?

I found myself murmuring a paraphrase of some lines from Shakespeare, in tribute to this awe-inspiring din:

> *Methought I heard a voice cry "Sleep no more!*
> *The Misses Winthrop do murder sleep," the*
> > *innocent sleep,*
> *Sleep that knits up the ravell'd sleave of care.*

We paused in the doorway of Prudence and Charity's bedroom, the servitors peeping over our shoulders.

"Charity, what *are* you doing? Prudence, it is Althea. Pray do not strike me with that broom."

"Mice! Hordes of them!" Charity paused in beating at the floor and walls with a pillow in order to answer me. Fido began barking and then pounced at a small moving shape.

Prudence said, "Our pillows are infested with their

nests! They creep between our sheets and swarm over the floor and up the draperies!"

"How remarkable!" I said. "I wonder why there should be such a sudden infestation. Fido, please be quiet. At any rate, you had best shift to another room to finish out the night. Perhaps . . . let me think . . . ah! This room at the end of the corridor—not too close to your old room, but in the same wing—I believe it has a large and relatively comfortable bed. May I assist you in moving?"

"No . . . no, we can manage, Althea," said Prudence. "Please go away, all of you."

"Are you certain?" I enquired. "I could bring your bedclothes, for instance. The bed coverings in the new room are sure to be cold and clammy."

"Ugh, no!" cried Charity. "I never want to so much as *look* at those bedclothes again. Disgusting!"

"But perhaps Annie could bring you a bedwarmer? No? Very well, if you are sure." Mama, Fido and I escorted them to their new domicile and, once they had inspected the bed for evidence of rodents and found none, we said goodnight and left them.

I did not lie down again. I feared it might take somewhat longer this time, and I preferred not to doze off. The nest of mice was under the wardrobe, in *this* room.

At least an hour must have passed before the screams

began anew. This time they more resembled wails than squeals; my stepsisters were grown tired and petulant.

"More vermin?" I asked at the doorway to their new room.

"They are everywhere! All the rooms are teeming with them!"

"Not quite," I said. "Mama and I have not been bothered in the east wing."

Prudence turned a suspicious gaze on me. "Oh? Not at all? That seems strange."

Charity, alerted by the tone of her sister's voice, looked around at that, and they both regarded me with narrowed eyes and scowling faces.

"Indeed, it seems odd to me also," I said. "I cannot think of an explanation—but wait! Perhaps I have it. Have you been eating, or storing, any food in your room?" Their hostile stares faltered, and they darted glances at one another out of the corners of their eyes.

"Oh, but what am I saying?" I went on, shaking my head at my own foolishness. "If you had bought any sweets or cakes or anything of that nature, you would have taken them to the kitchen, so that they could be served up to the entire household, rather than hiding them away. Forgive me for making such a suggestion. No, it must remain a mystery, I fear. However, there is a furnished room in our wing where you can sleep. Please allow me to show you."

They followed me in sulky silence to the preordained chamber in the east wing.

This time Fido and I climbed into bed and closed our eyes in well-deserved slumber. We slept so heavily that we almost missed the third disruption of the night when a fresh squall blew in across the sea from Norway and, lying as they were on a bed positioned under the worst of the leak in the roof, they began to feel the rain dripping onto their heads. I believe I may have heard a scream or two, but I did not bother to rouse myself. Rather, I snuggled down in my bed, with a satisfied smile on my face and a sense of accomplishment in my heart.

❧ ❧ ❧

It required several days of continued rain and marauding rodents before Prudence and Charity capitulated. When a fine cashmere shawl belonging to Prudence that had been left in their original bedchamber was found with holes chewed along the hem (I rather fancy that our maid, Annie, who had been encouraged to exaggerate the mouse problem, may have been involved), they demanded that *something* be done. Faced with our undeniable poverty, they had no option save to pay for that *something* themselves.

With much tsk-tsk-ing and fretful remarks about how we (my mother and I and, no doubt, my small brother and Fido as well) had allowed the castle to become so dilapidated that we had to rely on our too-trusting and too-easily-imposed-upon relations to keep it from falling into ruin, my stepsisters authorized the repairs and the extermination.

However, at last the rain was gone. The sun was come again, and so was the mason, to fix the roof this time. Happily, the repairs required proved to be minor rather than major. Also, a boy with a ferret was employed to clear out the infestation of mice. (I assisted in this latter task by removing the nests and their occupants to an unoccupied outbuilding.)

Mama was of course pleased, though surprised. "I can understand that they would wish to repair the roof, since they are now obliged to sleep in the leakiest bedroom, but it is a remarkable coincidence—" She looked at me and then down at her knitting, hiding a smile as she did so. "Never mind. Do not tell me. It is best I do not know."

Dutiful and loving daughter that I am, I honored her request, and changed the subject.

Now the rains were over, Lord Boring came calling again, renewing his suggestion that we get up a riding party. I was delighted at the prospect, save for one or two minor matters. The Baron would know by now that my dowry was small and our income only just equal to our maintenance, but I did not wish him to know how *very* tightly our purse was drawn.

Firstly, my riding habit was in tatters. And, while I was reasonably handy with my needle, ladies' riding habits were, like gentlemen's clothing, cut and sewn by skilled tailors. The expense of a professionally tailored riding jacket, let alone a smart hat to match, was not to be thought of. I began picking through our store of old linens and outgrown clothing, looking for something I could turn into a respectable piece of ladies' attire.

At last I came upon several suits of my father's, now very outdated in appearance. I was meditating upon the possibility of adapting them for Alexander's use someday, when an idea, full-formed, darted into my brain.

I have said that ladies' riding coats and jackets were traditionally tailored; they also were decidedly masculine in appearance, so that only a long skirt and sidesaddle posture gave away the sex of the rider from a distance.

Even the hats of fashionable ladies on horseback were inspired by military style.

When he was only sixteen my father had purchased a lieutenancy in the infantry in hopes of restoring his family fortune. These hopes ended at my grandfather's death, when my father was called home to manage the estate.

Here was a well-made, barely used uniform of an infantry lieutenant, the coat a brilliant red with shiny brass buttons, epaulettes, and a stand-up collar. The regulation hat was a shako, a handsome cylindrical affair with a visor and jaunty plumes.

Did I dare?

It was too large for me, of course, even tho' made for a boy of sixteen. However, if I carefully unpicked the seams, could I not take it in so it would fit? I decided that I could. I removed the white silk sash and several other insignia which too clearly indicated its provenance and began work. With a few hours' work, I had a close-fitting scarlet coatee that handsomely set off my black muslin skirt. (A white skirt might have seemed to mimic the official uniform a little *too* closely.) True, it was unusual for a woman to wear a coat of such a brilliant hue, but no one could deny that it was striking.

The hat was likewise a triumph. Once stripped of its gold cording and metal badge of rank, and then swaddled with a filmy black scarf, it became a very fashionable ladies' hat indeed. The feathers had been nibbled by moths, but a quick trim restored them. The only problem with the hat was that it was a bit large. I stuffed it with rags until it sat steady.

My attire for the outing now settled, I turned my attention to my second concern: my horse. She was an elderly mare who had to be coaxed up the smallest hill and suffered from severe vertigo on a rise of only a few feet. I dared not ride her near the cliffs. Once in recent months I had tried it; at first sight of the abyss she froze, her eyes grew large as saucers and in her terror she nearly plunged us both to our deaths. It would not do, not for her sake and not for mine.

The only way I could think of to obscure the fact that we could not afford a good ladies' riding horse for Mama and me was to pretend that my mare had been purchased for me as being extremely gentle. Actually she had only been extremely cheap, though she was a dear, good creature, named Pegeen. I was able to afford her maintenance largely due to the kindness of Sir Quentin, who regularly directed his farrier to attend to her, and incidentally sent along several bales of feed.

"Can't bear to see a horse badly shod," was his explanation.

I loved to ride—it was my passion—but I would have to behave like a nervous little miss too frightened to be mounted on anything more spirited than a child's hobbyhorse.

This was injurious to my pride, but I decided that it was for the best, at least for the moment. I could—could I not?—appear to *gradually* become more adventurous on horseback, so that by the wedding I would be so much at ease that His Lordship could give me a strong-willed Arabian stallion for the groom's gift to the bride. I closed my eyes and imagined myself galloping at a breakneck speed o'er hill and dale with the Baron at my side. However, if he was like most men, he would reserve the fiery stallion for himself and present me with a docile, younger version of Pegeen. Ah well, that was for the future.

I therefore decided that we would ride inland towards a group of megaliths arranged in a rough circle, known locally as "the Screaming Stones" because of the noise the wind made rushing between them. As standing stones went, they were not large or notable, but they were undeniably old, and might, by their extreme antiquity, provide a subject for reflection and conversation on the part of the more sensible members of the party and a certain amount of superstitious nonsense on the part of whichever of my stepsisters gained the right to accompany us.

Only one would be able to do so. My stepsisters had their own horse, shared between them. They would not on any account lend the animal so that Mama and I could ride together, or for any general purposes of the household, and would only allow it to be hitched to our chaise when *they* wished to be conveyed somewhere, such as on the night of the ball. Neither enjoyed riding much—the horse was for show and spent the vast majority of its life idle, eating its head off and growing stout—and so there was no reason to bear the expense of *two* when one was rarely used.

Once it occurred to Charity that she and Prudence would therefore not both be able to join the party, she proposed that we use the chaise.

"Then, you know, we could all go. It would be shocking to leave poor Mama Winthrop home," she said. As the younger of the two Winthrop daughters, *she* would be the one obliged to give way to her elder sister.

I shook my head. I, too, thought it would be a shame to leave my mother at home. But taking the chaise was not to be thought of. "The roads are far too bad. You know quite well that the last few miles of the way are nothing more than a track fit only for walking or riding. Of course, if you wished to take the chaise, leave it at

Allingham, and let Mama and me have the horses, while you and Prudence walked the rest of the way, it would certainly be very thoughtful and kind of y—"

"Certainly not!" "No, indeed!" cried Prudence and Charity.

Charity eyed me resentfully. At length she burst out, "I do not know why I should have to stay at home if Althea is to go. *She* is the youngest, after all. You ought to let me ride your horse, Althea. It's only right."

"Now, Charity," interposed my mother hastily, "I am sorry for your disappointment, but you know I will be grateful to have your company."

"*She* ought to stay at home. She is the youngest. I *want* her to lend me her horse." And Charity almost, but did not quite, stamp her foot.

"Charity, dear," said my mother, "Pegeen was purchased with funds from Althea's father's estate. He especially wished it—he even spoke of it on his deathbed—as Althea is so fond of riding. And you know that *you* have always been indifferent to the exercise. Pegeen is Althea's horse. Indeed, I am told that she leaves almost nothing for the stable boy to do, so far as caring for the animal."

"Perhaps, Charity," chimed in Prudence, "while we are disporting ourselves on the moors, you could get on with counting our lace handkerchiefs and other items of dress, before we send them out to the laundress? You have such an exquisite eye for detail."

Charity's face turned red and seemed to swell.

I had remained silent, but now I had to speak. The proper thing for me to do would be to offer my horse to her and remain at home. But I could not bear it. Charity and Prudence were both dreadful horsewomen, quick with the whip and heedless of the horse's comfort or safety. And the entire party had been a scheme of the Baron's so that *I* could show him the countryside.

"Charity—" I began, but at this tense moment Greengages shuffled into the room. "Mr. Fredericks, madam."

In strode Mr. Fredericks, the image of impatience. He nearly toppled poor Greengages onto the floor in his haste to enter, execute his business, and leave.

"Will two horses suffice, Mrs. Winthrop? If so, I will leave you. I've the devil of a lot of work to get through if I am to frivol away tomorrow chasing about after a collection of rocks in a circle. However, Boring insists that I attend."

"Mr. Fredericks, how do you do?" said my bewildered mama. "Which horses do you mean, sir?"

"Why, the ones that you, and one of your daughters, I suppose"—he looked about at us as though uncertain of *which* sex we were—"are to ride on the morrow. I am told you have not enough horseflesh to ensure that everyone will be able to ride. Boring thought we ought to send a few over on loan."

I could feel a flush of gratification rising to my cheeks. *This* was a marked attention, without mistake. He must have meant this to give me pleasure, and it was a thoughtful, generous gesture. True, I could have wished His Lordship had come to offer the horses himself instead of allowing his boorish friend to deliver them. However, perhaps he felt too self-conscious to appear in person.

I smiled and said nothing as my mother, with a swift glance at me, agreed that two horses would be adequate. Mr. Fredericks declined to sit down or accept refreshment and was gone, having been in the room for something less than five minutes.

"Never mind, Althea," said Charity. "I had much, much rather ride the Baron's horse than your poor old thing."

Since I too had much, much rather she ride the Baron's horse than my poor old thing, I said nothing but merely smiled.

8

THE DAY OF OUR trip to the Screaming Stones dawned early, as it does in June in northern England: at about half past the hour of four in the morning, in fact. No matter how near dawn came to the time that we had laid our heads down on our pillows the night before, Fido and Alexander felt that we ought to be up and active if the sun was over the horizon. There was no lying abed until noon, as I am told fine London ladies are in the habit of doing—at least, not for Mama and me, who must see to the details of our excursion.

It gave every promise of a lovely day, with not a cloud to be seen. In the midst of preparations I paused a moment by the stables to study the sky (the outlook was excellent, the groom who was readying the horses assured me). My gaze dropped to the castle with its mad, eccentric towers and buttresses, and beyond to the land where I lived. The groom, who was an intelligent, good sort of man, whose family had worked for mine for many generations, noticed my thoughtful look and said, smiling, "T'castle be a rare fine place, mistress."

"Jock, it is," I agreed. I knew that he and I felt much the same loyalty to Crooked Castle. "And it *must* be kept in the family. It must be preserved for Master Alexander."

"Aye, mistress, that it must," he said, and then began talking about provisions for the day.

I had begun to think of our journey as something more than a mere pleasure jaunt; rather, it resembled a military sortie in our campaign to keep the castle. I believed that Jock shared my view. If ever we were forced to abandon our home it would go hard not only on us, but on our tenants and servants as well. They knew it, and I knew that they were looking to me to protect their homes and livelihood with a good marriage. Beyond my immediate family, thirty-seven people (give or take a few babies) were anxiously waiting to see how I would dispose of my hand in matrimony.

I thought of the Baron's handsome face and figure and felt that I could resign myself to doing my duty quite cheerfully if only I were given the chance to do so.

Mrs. Westing and Mrs. Fredericks had sent their regrets at not attending our little party, feeling that the expedition would require them to travel both for a longer time and over rougher roads than either was accustomed to on horseback. I was sorry for this, as I wished to be better acquainted with Lord Boring's mother, and as *my* mother so enjoyed the conversation of Mrs. Fredericks. And besides, if Mrs. Fredericks had come to keep Mama company I should have had no compunction about leaving her alone from time to time in order to walk with his Lordship.

Our nuncheon was not to be anything grand. I had looked in the larder and found a great many shriveled parsnips and other, less identifiable roots left over from last fall. After I had boiled these for an hour or two and added some currants and sugar, I encased the result in pastry, baked it, and called it a pie. The vegetable garden yielded herbs enough for a green salad, with the addition of some wild sorrel and dandelion leaves. That would have to suffice. It was packed up in Jock's saddlebags— Lord Boring had not forgotten to send over a pony for him so that he could wait upon us and see to the horses while we strolled about the countryside. I lingered to supervise the careful packing of two of those few bottles of wine that remained to us of what had once been a fine wine cellar, as well as a cool jug of barley water.

"I want to go! I want to go, too, 'Leetha!" Alexander burst out of the door, trotting on his little-boy legs as fast as he could, with Mama in pursuit. Fido, who was, as always, at my heels, began to bark and prance about the child, twisting in ridiculous, hysterical circles and adding to Alexander's uproar.

I sighed. I had known that these two would be distraught if excluded from our party, but could not see how to include them. I said, "Mama, if you could see to it that Prudence and Charity are up, and that they are ready on time, I will take Alexander out to the garden where we can throw the ball for Fido." If I could exhaust their busy little bodies prior to our departure, it might make it easier to consign them both to Annie's care.

For at least an hour I played with them, running and throwing the ball until I felt that I, at least, would prefer to go back to my chamber and fall into an exhausted slumber rather than set out on an eight-mile ride over rough country. At the end of that time Mama appeared and signaled to me that we were nearly ready to depart. My companions shifted their shining eyes from my face to hers.

"I—I am coming," I gasped. I hurried indoors and donned my "new" riding habit. Fido and Alexander, showing no sign of fatigue, followed me out to the stable yard where the others had assembled.

Lord Boring, the Marquis of Bumbershook and the inevitable Mr. Fredericks were present, already mounted, as were my mother and stepsisters. The latter two stared suspiciously at my habit, knowing my wardrobe every bit as well as I did.

"Where did *that* come from?" Charity demanded.

"What, this old thing?" I said, "Goodness, it's been around forever."

"It's *red*," said Prudence. "And that hat! It reminds me of a—"

"Are we all ready? Althea, do come along now," interrupted my mother. A tiny smile told me that she had guessed the origin of my new garb. Jock stood holding his pony and my Pegeen in readiness for me to mount. Annie was there to see us off and take charge of boy and dog. When Alexander spotted his friend Mr. Fredericks, however, his face lit up. "Freddicks!" he cried, and trotted towards him, his arms held up to be lifted. "I want to come!" he demanded.

We gasped in dismay and Annie and I, the only adults present on foot who were not encumbered by horses, hurried towards him. Mr. Fredericks was mounted on a fine bay that danced with impatience to be gone, disliking the proximity of this small, unsteady human.

Mr. Fredericks laid a hand on the horse's neck. "Be still," he said, and the animal quieted and stood immobile. Then he leaned over and casually snatched my brother up with one hand by the scruff of his jacket. "So you want to come too, do you?" Alexander nodded, giggling at being manhandled. "Then you shall," said Mr. Fredericks.

"Fredericks!" Lord Boring said.

"Yes?"

"The boy's mother has some say in the matter."

"Has she?" Mr. Fredericks considered this. "Well, perhaps she has. Is she—yes, there she is. Do you object, madam?"

If he had said this in a superior or dismissive tone of voice, I believe I should have rushed at him without heed for his powerful horse and snatched Alexander from him. But he did not. He spoke in a tone of apparently genuine enquiry.

"I—I hadn't thought—but I suppose it would be all right—"

"Fredericks," growled the Marquis. "The lady is distressed."

"No . . . no," my mother went on in a stronger voice, "Truly, Your Lordship, I would not object, if Mr. Fredericks keeps a tight hold of him, and does not . . . *forget* that the child is riding with him."

Mr. Fredericks's eyebrows shot up to his hairline. He seemed offended. "Forget? Forget that my good friend

Alexander has claimed my care and protection? Certainly not."

Oddly enough, for my mama was the most loving and careful mother in existence, this appeared to satisfy her. "Very well," she said, "you shall come, Alexander. Mind you do not cause Mr. Fredericks a moment of annoyance. Althea? Are you ready?"

Bemused, I turned without a word. Jock was at hand with Pegeen, bent over to boost me into the saddle. I was mounted and ready to leave when another disturbance occurred. I became aware of something clinging to my ankle. Poor old Pegeen shied at the discovery that a small dog was attempting to claw itself up her flank onto my lap.

I heard a shout of laughter; Mr. Fredericks was amused at my plight. "You may as well bring him, you know. The boy and the dog will keep an eye on one another, and the dog will only follow you if you leave him behind."

"I suppose you are right," I admitted. I leant down and pulled Fido the rest of the way up, much relieving Pegeen. "Lie down and be still," I ordered the dog.

Conscious of having got their way against great odds, and wise enough to appreciate it, neither interloper did anything more than look about with wide, delighted eyes all the long eight miles from Crooked Castle to the Screaming Stones. I kept a sharp eye on Mr. Fredericks, but he was as good as his word and held fast to my brother, lowering his head to speak with him from time to time.

The day grew warmer. My hat, made of leather and felt and padded with rags, began to seem oppressively hot, and as the track grew rougher it tipped precariously from one side of my head to the other with increasing frequency. An unexpected sensation on the back of my neck made me realize that half the stuffing had slipped out and was fluttering in the wind behind me. I hastily pushed it back inside and crammed the chapeau down over my forehead. Fashionable or no, it was beginning to seem a great inconvenience. I wondered how soldiers could bear wearing the great, heavy things, in addition to all the other hardships of military life.

As we neared our goal, several intensely green patches surrounding what appeared to be small ponds became visible. I pointed them out to Lord Boring, who had shown an amiable tendency to ride alongside me the whole way, slowing his horse's pace to match Pegeen's.

"It looks like a good spot to water the horses," he observed.

"That is what I feared you might think, my lord," I

replied. "And it is a dangerous idea, I am sorry to say. They are not shallow ponds but rather flooded mine shafts which drop off immediately to a depth of sixty or so feet. A thin mat of vegetation fringes the rim, giving the false impression of solid ground over what is really a subaquatic void. It is a shocking dereliction of responsibility on the part of the mine owners not to cover them. A stranger to the area such as yourself might allow his horse to wade in for a drink and quite likely neither horse nor man would ever be seen again. But few strangers venture here, and so I suppose they think their laxity justified."

"I see," he said, smiling. "How fortunate I am to have your advice and guidance before exploring on my own. May I add," he went on in a lower tone, leaning towards me to speak words meant for me alone, "that I could wish that I might always enjoy that benefit."

I was silent for a moment, waiting—we seemed close to a declaration and a formal proposal of marriage—but he said nothing further. I therefore responded demurely, "I am always pleased to be of service to a neighbor," and continued, "Another such flooded pit lies quite close to the Screaming Stones. It is not safe to approach on foot or on horseback. Perhaps you could ride ahead and warn the others, before someone tumbles in."

"Yes indeed," he said, and urged his horse on to catch up with the others. It obeyed with alacrity, no doubt glad to break out into a trot, instead of the slow amble that Pegeen's age and infirmities forced upon us.

The stones were now visible, standing up on the brow of a hill in relief against the sky, like the teeth of some monstrous carnivore. Tho' we have become so enlightened and sophisticated in this modern age, the primitive monument still had the power to halt the whole party in its tracks, allowing me to catch them up.

At this moment a gust of wind blew across the moor and played amongst the monoliths, which were long boulders stood on end pointing skywards, an expression of pre-Christian religious beliefs. A high, piping sound began to be heard, which within moments deepened into a lugubrious wolf's howl. The horses, independently of their riders' direction, bunched together in a defensive position, their nostrils flaring, testing the wind for danger. Even my stepsisters fell silent.

"Egad," said the Marquis, impressed. "D'you suppose the fellows that set these stones in place knew what a racket they would make?"

"I often think that they wanted to give the wind a voice," said Mama softly.

"Well, dear lady, it appears that the wind has some

beastly unpleasant things to say," said the Marquis, laughing uneasily.

"It fair makes my skin crawl," agreed Lord Boring. "What a singularly desolate place this is."

As if in agreement, the pitch of the stones' complaint rose into a scream. I was beginning to regret my suggestion that we make this destination our object. Certainly it was hardly the right atmosphere for romantic dalliance.

Prudence, evidently thinking it incumbent upon her to depress the spirits of the party still further, remarked, "I am always reminded by these awe-inspiring stones of the dreadful hand of Death"—Prudence could be reminded of the dreadful hand of Death by such varied events as a tradesman's call, a broken fingernail, or a skylark singing out on the moor—"and of Horace's lines: 'Years, following years, steal something every day; / At last they steal us from ourselves away.'"

"Thank you, Prudence," I said.

Mr. Fredericks, alone of the gentlemen, had said nothing, and I looked at him to observe his reaction. His eyes, I noted with foreboding, were alight with speculation and interest.

"I don't know—it's jolly interesting. I wonder how they raised those monstrous big stones up without a block and tackle," he said. "And what *keeps* them up? If only one had brought a shovel . . ." and he urged his horse into a canter towards the circle of stones.

I gave Pegeen a good hard nudge and went after him with as much speed as she could muster.

"*Mr. Fredericks!*" I cried, when I was again in earshot, "Those stones have stood on this hill for several millennia, and the people hereabouts have strong feelings about them. I do not want to have to explain my carelessness in exposing them to your curiosity without exacting the strictest promise that you shall not be allowed to molest them or touch them in any way."

"*I? I* promise not to molest them? I assure you, madam—"

"The only assurance I require, Mr. Fredericks, is that you will not lay a hand anywhere on even one of these stones," I said in a steely tone. "*Mr. Fredericks!*" He was dismounting, gripping Alexander with one hand and the pommel of his saddle with the other. I gasped in alarm, but they were safely down. Jock trotted hastily up on his pony and took charge of the bay.

"Oh, very well, I shan't," Mr. Fredericks said sulkily. "I would just like to have tried . . ."

"Remember! You have given your word," I said. Clutching Fido, I managed to dismount.

Mr. Fredericks heaved a loud sigh, held up his hands

for my inspection, and then thrust them into his pockets.

"Ha! Fredericks, you have met your mistress!" said the Marquis as he climbed down and joined us.

"You're right," Lord Boring agreed. "I don't believe I've ever known a lady who could make Fredericks mind his manners before. Or a gentleman either, save you and I, Bumbershook, on occasion. I am astounded."

Mr. Fredericks paid no attention to this chaffing. He was still fascinated by the engineering feat presented by the stones, which were nearly seven feet in height. Keeping his hands in his pockets he circled one stone. He stopped, poked at the base with the toe of his boot, then slid his gaze over to judge the expression on my face.

"Mr. Fredericks," I said. "I believe you agreed not to touch them in any way?"

He heaved another sigh. Alexander, who was growing bored with the stone circle, tugged at his arm. "Come on, Freddicks," he said, and Mr. Fredericks allowed himself to be escorted away from the megaliths. I thankfully discarded the hateful hat and followed them.

9

WHILE JOCK BUSIED HIMSELF setting out the picnic nuncheon, we took a stroll around the area. The party broke up into groupings that I had not anticipated. Alexander was unwilling to relinquish the company of his friend Mr. Fredericks, and, as it seemed to me only proper that the gentleman who was responsible for Alexander's presence should also be responsible for entertaining him, I was content with this pairing.

Prudence, who still cherished ambitions with regard to Mr. Fredericks, requested that he lend her an arm to guide her over the rough ground and, after one blank look, he complied gracefully enough. I must own that I admired her courage. I hoped she would neither find herself steered into a bog hole nor break an ankle falling into a badger's sett.

The Marquis offered his arm to my mother, and I soon had the happiness of seeing them laughing and talking together quite like old friends. I looked around for

Lord Boring, only to discover that Charity had swooped in and carried him off. They were already some distance away, His Lordship looking back over his shoulder and Charity tugging him along, setting quite a smart pace in her urgency to remove him from my vicinity.

In short, I was left alone and desolate. As the group included only *three* grown-up gentlemen and *four* ladies, it was inevitable that two ladies would have to share, but I had not anticipated having to make do with no gentle-man at all. Rather chagrinned at this development after all my fine plans for the day, I decided to walk behind Mr. Fredericks and Prudence, the better to keep an eye on my brother. Though I knew that my mother would be watching as well, she was distracted by the attentions of the Marquis, and I reasoned that if I could not advance my own cause at present, I could at least allow her to enjoy a conversation with an intelligent, educated adult in peace.

Alexander had been most strongly warned against re-moving his shoes, dirtying his stockings, wandering off alone, climbing any of the few trees that dotted the land-scape, and, with a good deal of emphasis, going anywhere near the flooded mine shaft. So far as the caution against the old tin mine went, I had warned him, Mama had warned him, and Lord Boring had warned him, all within

Mr. Fredericks's hearing. This being the case, I was not surprised to find that Mr. Fredericks and Alexander were making straight for it, ignoring Prudence's pleas to pause for a moment to admire a large gorse bush in full flower.

I had expected this and forbore to comment, but waited while the two gentlemen, large and small, walked at a safe distance around the mine shaft thrice. Satisfied, they obediently returned to look at the gorse bush.

If you have ever been on the English moors in early June you will be aware that a gorse plant in bloom, while a reasonably attractive object, is hardly a rarity. The moor does not offer a great deal of variety of flowering plants. Heather has a purple blossom; gorse has a yellow. When in bloom, nearly every vista that is not a vast sweep of purple is therefore a vast sweep of yellow, or an admixture of both.

The gorse bush is the taller of the two, and covered with a great many sharp green spikes. If you keep in mind that most of the flowers are, at any given moment, being visited by a variety of stinging insects in search of pollen, it will be clear to you that a gorse bush is an object to be treated with respect. It would not, for instance, be wise to begin reciting the gloomier poetry of Robert Herrick ("And this same flower that smiles today / Tomorrow will be dying") next to one, at least not if you insist on swinging your parasol rhythmically about by way of accompaniment to your lyrical effusions.

This is what Prudence did, however. The energetic, slashing movements of her arm disturbed not one but several bees, which expressed their disapproval either of her literary tastes or, more likely, her style of elocution, by stinging her all at once.

She shrieked, and in her haste to escape their attentions, tripped and fell into the bush. This annoyed the other bees and, while some chose a dignified retreat to other, less agitated gorse bushes, a goodly number mounted an offensive against poor Prudence, who was thrashing about, unable to flee, since her clothing was caught up on the thorns.

I hurried to Prudence's side, commanding Mr. Fredericks, who was standing and gawking at the spectacle, to assist me at once. The sting of a bee, while painful, is usually not a serious matter. However, many stings all sustained at once might be of more concern, and I have heard that some unfortunate persons have an acute sensitivity to bee venom.

I will say for Mr. Fredericks that, once I demanded his assistance in no uncertain terms, he proved quick and efficient. He grasped Prudence without ceremony by the elbows and lifted. With several sharp twists that reminded me of the removal of a wine cork, he disengaged her skirt and pelisse from the green spines of the gorse bush, carried her some ten or fifteen feet away, and set her down.

Whereupon she fainted.

The rest of our party had been alerted to the mishap and converged upon the stricken lady with offers of harts-horn and wine to revive her. These had their effect, and soon she was propped up against my knee being fanned by her sister. The stings were beginning to swell, but Jock was able to supply some vinegar that had been meant as a dressing for the salad, and this soothed them somewhat.

After a passage of some minutes it was clear that Prudence was *not* one of those with an acute sensitivity to bee venom, and we all became more composed and started having thoughts about food. With the Baron's assistance, Prudence even managed to rise from the ground and take a few tottering steps towards the vicinity where our meal had been laid out.

"*Where is Alexander?*"

It was my mother's voice, and I looked about in sudden terror.

No small boy was anywhere in sight. Neither, I realized, was a small dog within view.

"Alexander! Fido! Where are you?" I cried.

My mother, whose face had turned snow-white, lifted her skirts and ran, calling out for my brother, with the Marquis close behind her. Prudence found herself abandoned, left to dab vinegar on her injuries in fretful solitude as the others scattered, searching. Some hastened to the other side of the hill, some to a copse of trees nearby, some went hunting amongst the standing stones, which chose that moment to resume their eerie, mournful song.

I stood still a moment, thinking. When I lifted my eyes they met Mr. Fredericks's.

"The tin mine," we said in unison.

Mr. Fredericks, unencumbered by skirts and delicate shoes, was the faster of the two of us, and I motioned him ahead. "Go. Go! Make haste!"

Oh, the sight that greeted us at the old tin mine! A pathetic pile of discarded clothing several feet off from the brink and a faint, a very, very faint disturbance in the waters.

Heedful of my warning about the fragility of the edges, Mr. Fredericks knelt down and crawled towards the pool on his hands and knees. Groping about with one hand while supporting himself with the other he succeeded in catching hold of *something* in the water. Yet no sooner had he grasped it than the ground beneath him crumbled and he too pitched into the mine headfirst.

After an agonizing moment, *three* heads—two human and one canine—appeared above the surface, gasped for air and then disappeared again.

"Oh!" I cried. "What shall I do?" Looking wildly about, my eyes fell on a tree branch of considerable size lying some distance off beside its parent tree. "Help me, help me," I screamed as I began to drag the heavy, cumbersome thing towards the mine shaft. "Oh, will no one come?"

No one did come, for they were out of earshot. The baleful shriek of the stone circle drowned out my pleas for assistance; the old gods were seemingly hungry for a blood sacrifice. At last I managed to half-pull and half-roll the limb to the edge. I had learned by Mr. Fredericks's mistake and did not approach closer than six feet until I had pushed the tree limb, first with my hands and then by sitting on the ground and kicking with my feet, into a position athwart the mine. Supported on two banks, it spanned a portion of the water.

A hand appeared above the water and grasped the branch. A head surfaced—it was Mr. Fredericks's—and then another. Alexander! Both sputtered and coughed; both were indubitably alive.

"Fido!" I cried in despair. "My Fido!"

But my cry of grief was unnecessary, for there he was,

crawling up onto Mr. Fredericks's shoulder, attempting to bark with his lungs half full of water. Weeping with joy I fell to my knees.

Still, work was yet to be done and no one to do it but myself. From a supine position and placing most of my weight on the branch, I slowly and cautiously crept out until I could touch the sodden group. Fido got his claws on the branch and sprang up onto my back and hence onto the shore. He had pushed off with such vigor from Mr. Fredericks's shoulder, however, that the remaining two were submerged again, tho' briefly.

Coughing (Alexander) and cursing (Mr. Fredericks), they reappeared and, after catching their breaths, Mr. Fredericks proposed handing Alexander off to me. I reached out my arms for him. By rolling painfully on my side over the tree bough with the child in my arms, I at length deposited him on firm earth.

Alexander vomited up a good deal of water, and afterward we lay, panting, for some long moments.

"My apologies for interrupting your meditations, madam, but I am still awaiting my extraction from this pit, where, I might add, I find myself as a result of going to the rescue of *your* brother and dog."

Even while behaving like a hero, Mr. Fredericks's manners were detestable.

I gripped Alexander to my breast again and rolled some few feet further away from the mine shaft. This time he was recovered enough to complain that I was crushing him, but I paid no mind. I sat him down on a boulder and fetched his clothing.

"Put those on," I ordered. "And if you, or Fido," I fixed them both with my eye, "stir so much as an inch until I tell you that you may do so, you will be instantly turned to stone."

I then turned my attention back to Mr. Fredericks.

"How long can you hold on, sir?" I enquired. "I fear I have not the strength to pull you out unaided."

A loud, aggrieved sigh could be heard issuing from the pool.

"Oh, I imagine I can hang on as long as need be. Why you couldn't pay enough attention to the lad to prevent this from occurring, I *don't* know. However, if you will take these boots from me—they are confoundedly heavy. I feel as though they're dragging me down to Hades."

There came a great deal of thrashing around in the water as Mr. Fredericks struggled to get his boots off one-handed. I soon found myself receiving first one and then another large, waterlogged Hessian.

"Be careful of those," Mr. Fredericks instructed, having thrust the second boot square into my face. "They cost a monstrous sum of money. No, don't *throw* them, you'll scratch the leather."

"Mr. Fredericks, I cannot imagine how you can worry about scratching the leather on a pair of boots at a moment like this!"

"I tell you they were dashed expensive," he said. "Boring brought me to this little shop on Bond Street and you would not credit the price they demanded— Here, make that animal go away!"

A stray sheep, stimulated by this unexpected excitement in a normally placid life, had approached unobserved and was preparing to sniff at Mr. Fredericks's head. I shooed it away before it could fall into the mine as well. Fido leapt to his feet with intent to give pursuit, but at a command from me sat down again.

"And why *you*, Fido," I added, pursuing a grievance which had been weighing on my mind, "had to go and fall in on top of Alexander, I am quite at a loss to determine."

"By heavens, you're ungrateful!" said Mr. Fredericks. "The dog knows you're fond of the boy and he was merely trying to fetch him back for you. He almost lost his life in the process."

"I don't see why he could not have barked. I—" Here our squabble was interrupted by the sound of my mother's voice.

"*Alexander!*"

At last. I heaved a grateful sigh. We were discovered.

Mama snatched up my brother into a clasp so tight it made him cry out. The others soon followed, stories were recounted and methods for rescuing Mr. Fredericks debated. After listening to this for some minutes the gentleman himself began to issue orders.

"You, Mrs. Hrm . . . Alexander's mother. You take the boy and get him to someplace warm and dry. Bumbershook, you'd better escort her. Then you, the one who fell into the gorse bush, and the other one, the sister, you go home, as you are of no use here. Your groom can look after you and make sure you don't get lost. Boring can go to Allingham, or to the nearest farm, and get some rope and some farm hands with which to hoist me out. *She*"—he jerked his chin in my direction—"can stay here and feed me something sustaining whilst I am hanging here like a trussed chicken in a stockpot ready for the boiling."

"Oh, but it would not be proper *at all* to leave Althea here alone with a gentleman not related to her," protested Prudence. (I suspect she had not cared for being referred to as "the one who fell into the gorse bush" and adjudged to be "of no use" after having taken pains to walk with him.)

I, however, had had time to think over the plan. "But

there *is* no one else, Prudence, and we cannot leave the gentleman who nearly sacrificed his life for little Alexander alone to his fate. Unless of course, you wish to stay—"

"No, indeed! I believe I have suffered quite enough on this expedition, without sacrificing my reputation."

My mother was already being helped up onto her horse. Lord Bumbershook handed Alexander up to her. "Never mind, Prudence," she called. "It will only be for a moment at most. The Marquis has spotted smoke from a chimney just over those trees. They will not be long unchaperoned."

"Unchaperoned!" said Mr. Fredericks testily. "I'd like to know what outrages to this young lady's modesty anyone thinks I am capable of administering, under the circumstances."

It occurred to me that he was more than capable of outraging my modesty even under these circumstances, by insisting on disrobing even further than he already had. "I have changed my mind," I said. "Mama, pray ask Charity to remain with me. She can ride home with us once Mr. Fredericks is freed."

Prudence raised objections, but Charity agreed with hardly a murmur. I suppose she was imagining riding home side by side with the Baron while I was distracted by my care for Mr. Fredericks.

In a few moments everyone save we three had ridden off. Considering the number of events that had occurred since we had arrived at the Screaming Stones, it was an astonishing fact that the sun had only advanced a few degrees towards the horizon.

"I'm hungry," Mr. Fredericks reminded me.

We investigated the uneaten food left for us by Jock.

"Althea, I pray you, do not touch anything. You are most dreadfully wet and dirty," said Charity, making a little *moue* of distaste. "And you have dead plants in your hair."

Mr. Fredericks could be heard laughing in the mine shaft. "You are indeed a spectacle, Miss Hrrm. I did not like to say so, but really, you ought to see the condition of your face."

I lost my temper.

"My name is *Miss Crawley*, Mr. Fredericks. My mother's name is *Mrs. Winthrop*, the young lady who fell into the gorse bush is *Miss Winthrop* and her younger sister, the lady beside me, is named *Miss Charity Winthrop*. I will thank you to remember and use our proper names when you address us. We, as well as males like yourself and your friends and my brother, Alexander, are thinking and feeling creatures deserving of courtesy and recognition.

"And I should like to point out that it was largely on your authority that Master Alexander was included on this outing, and that you swore that once Alexander had claimed your care and protection, you would *never let him down*."

"Oh," said the voice from the mine shaft, and then fell silent.

And remained silent for the remaining half an hour until the rescuers arrived, during which time I fed him half of the pie (he gave the contents of this pastry several sharp looks, but said nothing—I find that sugar reconciles the palate to most things) and administered several draughts of barley water. He barely uttered a sound while enduring what I am sure was a most uncomfortable extraction process, and did not speak at all on the long, long ride home over the eight miles of rough road.

10

WAS I EMBARRASSED BY my lack of control over my emotions and my tongue? No, certainly not. Mr. Fredericks's bad behavior had earned my scorn and open condemnation.

Of course, on the other hand, he had saved my brother's life. I loved my brother dearly, and this man had risked his own life to rescue Alexander. So yes, I was mortified by my own behavior. Dreadfully so, the more I thought of it.

But he had saved my brother's life only after first endangering it. He had promoted Alexander's presence on the trip without any consideration of our mother's wishes. And . . . oh, in general, he was so rude and inconsiderate!

Still, he had undergone great discomfort for the sake of my brother. Not, of course, without a number of complaints, but yet . . .

In the weeks that followed our ill-fated journey to the

Screaming Stones, I would have been glad to exchange my mind for almost anyone else's. I grew so weary of trying to judge who was in the right that I could happily have changed lots with a turnip or a cabbage.

I was not called upon to speak to the unspeakable Mr. Fredericks again, as he abruptly went away to London—on business, Lord Boring explained. Perhaps His Lordship had sent him away, perhaps even because he knew how I disliked his cousin. However, perhaps not. If he was Lord Boring's man of business, he must have had to go away to tend to that business from time to time instead of merely adding up sums in his offices at Gudgeon Park and otherwise lolling about eating and drinking at his cousin's expense.

And London being so far away, I had hopes that I should not have to entertain Mr. Fredericks again any time soon. After much fruitless soul-searching I banished all thought of him from my mind and fixed it upon its proper object: the Baron. Oh, and also the Marquis, as that pleasant gentleman continued his stay at the Park and seemed to consider it a matter of course to accompany the Baron whenever he chanced to call on us.

I still believed that a marriage so grand as one to the Marquis was beyond my grasp, and in truth, I should have been sorry to be the means of causing a rift in the friendship enjoyed between the Marquis and the Baron. So obvious were the attentions the Baron had paid me that I could not imagine how the Marquis could court me without putting that relationship in danger. In any case, I enjoyed his company, and he amused my mother.

Although my high hopes for the outing to the Screaming Stones had ended in near disaster and no progress at all so far as coming to a better understanding with Lord Boring, I had assumed that that understanding would not be slow in coming. I was wrong. Lord Boring continued to be all that was delightful and charming but did not again speak of wishing that I might be in a position to provide advice and guidance on a more permanent basis than might be expected from a mere neighbor.

Part of the trouble no doubt lay with his mother. She rarely called with him at the castle, and when we called upon her, her manner to me and to my mother was distant. She quickly abandoned us to the company of Mrs. Fredericks, preferring to lay out rows of cards in an endless game of patience and ignore our presence. Clearly she was not anxious to see me as her daughter-in-law. My family and lineage were quite good enough—Crawleys had married into the lower ranks of the aristocracy often enough in the past that I should not be thought unsuitable on that account. And I could not see any reason for her to dislike or disapprove of me, based upon my manners or reputation. Indeed, she had hardly been in company with me often enough to have formed a prejudice against me. It could therefore only be my fortune, or lack of it, that persuaded her to regard me with disapprobation.

But why should that be a factor? The refurbishment of Gudgeon Park was on such a lavish scale (indeed, Mrs. Fredericks was so much engaged in this work that my mother complained she rarely saw her) that I could not help but assume money was in plentiful supply. However, a large fortune is so commonly married off to a similarly large fortune that I suppose the feeling is that one cannot have too much of a good thing.

One morning both gentlemen appeared at the castle with the news that guests were soon expected at the Park.

"Mother's friends, the Vincys," explained Lord Boring.

"Mr., Mrs., and *Miss* Vincy," added the Marquis, lifting his eyebrows at the *Miss*.

"Oh?" I said, on the alert, "And what sort of a young lady is Miss Vincy?"

Lord Boring's handsome face flushed. "A devilish plain one," he said.

The Marquis shook his head at his friend. "You are less than gallant, Boring. She is a very pleasant young lady."

"You are right. My apologies," said Lord Boring, and changed the subject.

❧ ❧ ❧

Prudence, Charity, and I happened to be in Lesser Hoo purchasing a bolt of figured muslin when they arrived in the village. Fido barked as a strange coach came to a halt in the inn yard.

At first sight we concluded that it was made of solid gold. Two footmen, attired in emerald velvet with scarlet piping and powdered white wigs, dismounted from the glittering equipage and enquired the way to Gudgeon Park. Old Owens, the ostler at the inn, gawked at this splendor for a few moments, then gathered up his scattered wits and pointed out their proper route without a word. Before the coach disappeared I spotted a veiled face peering out of the window and the gleam of two curious eyes.

"Well!" said Charity. "It couldn't have been made of gold, of course. Do you suppose it could have been *gilded?*"

"You couldn't!" objected Prudence. "It would wear

off. People—stable boys and so on—would scrape it off and sell it."

"It *looked* like gold." They argued about it for some time, eventually coming to an agreement that whatever the material was, it was a most vulgar and ostentatious display.

"Did you notice the *shoes* the footman was wearing?" asked Charity.

Prudence nodded her head slowly up and down. "I did."

"I would do almost anything for a pair of slippers like that," said her sister.

"I know," agreed Prudence, and the two of them stared resentfully down the road after the coach, irritated beyond words at the fact that their own shoes were not half so finely made as a footman's. A vulgar and ostentatious display, indeed.

We abandoned our shopping expedition and instead filled the market basket with wild blackberries we gathered by the side of the road. These provided a pretext to call at Gudgeon Park, and as we happened to espy Mama and Alexander crossing a field on our way, they joined us. When Mama, upon being seated in the drawing room, realized that the purpose of our call was to inspect newcomers who had not yet had the chance to shake the dust of the road from their garments, she shook her head at me. However, she was quite pleased to have the chance herself. The comings and goings of a great house like Gudgeon Park could not help but be a prime source of entertainment in a small, rural neighborhood like Lesser Hoo.

Mr. Vincy proved to be a short, stout, bald person with sharp little button eyes and a common way of speaking that made it obvious that his money came from trade rather than inheritance. Indeed, it almost made me giddy to think how *much* money he must have made through commerce, to be received as an honored guest in these sacred precincts. He spoke little, except for expressing regret that Mr. Fredericks should have left so abruptly, and so soon before their arrival. Evidently the two men had shared business interests.

"That Fredericks, he's a rare 'un," said Mr. Vincy, shaking his head in apparent admiration. "Never have known anyone to beat him. He's a wonder, all right."

No one present had any reason to contradict this statement, and so the conversation was turned to other subjects.

Mrs. Vincy was also short and stout but possessed an accent so refined and a voice so high and nasal that she sounded as if she were calling an infantry division to order on a bugle, rather than merely wishing us a good morning. Mr. Vincy had managed to marry *up* on the social scale. She was, Mrs. Westing hastened to explain, the former Miss Babbage of Hurling Hall in Essex. Her dress was rather reminiscent of her carriage: it appeared to have been dipped in liquid silver and then studded all over with pearls, like raisins on a plum pudding. It was far more appropriate for a ballroom than for traveling, or even for such a fine drawing room as the one at Gudgeon Park at two o'clock in the afternoon.

Miss Vincy was . . . Miss Vincy was plain. Very plain. In the middle twenties, past her first youth, she had skin badly pitted with smallpox scars, and she could not have been a beauty even before the disease disfigured her. She wore a fine lace scarf wrapped around her head, obscuring her face. From time to time her mother leaned forward and adjusted this so that it cast her still more into the shade.

"My daughter," she said in her high, piping voice, "is most *dreadfully* prone to colds."

I nodded and agreed that she was wise to wrap her up warmly, even though her daughter was sitting by a fire on a hot day in July.

My good mama, who was sitting next to Miss Vincy, began quietly conversing with her, enquiring about their journey, her family's friendship with Mrs. Westing, and her interests and daily pursuits. Miss Vincy admitted that she was fond of drawing, which naturally led to a request to see her sketchbook, and they were soon leafing through pages of her impressions of the road from London to Yorkshire. Prudence, who considered herself an expert by virtue of her representations of mourning urns and weeping willows, leaned over their shoulders and offered criticisms.

At last Miss Vincy became animated enough that her scarf fell back and revealed her entire face. Her mother, noticing, leaned forward to lift it back up again, but was prevented.

"Please, Mother," Miss Vincy murmured. "It is so *hot* in here, I cannot bear it." Her mother darted a swift glance at Lord Boring. In a yet lower voice, so low I could barely hear it, Miss Vincy added, "He *knows* what I look like."

"Yes, but," her mother retorted with a venomous look at me, "he had no one with whom to compare you earlier." This was spoken loud enough that Mama and I could not even pretend not to hear.

Miss Vincy leaned away from her mother and tucked the scarf into the neckline of her dress. "No woman could be ashamed of being outshone by Miss Crawley, Mother," she said in a quiet but carrying voice. "I hope it will not embarrass her if I say that I think she is quite the most beautiful creature I have ever seen. I should very much like to paint her portrait."

I thanked her, and, on her mother moving away for a moment, took the opportunity to go and sit next to her and join in the examination of her artwork.

"Oh, how lovely! You are very talented. Look how clever this drawing of the children is! And this stretch of moor and mountain—it's beautiful," I cried, delighted by lively scenes captured from the windows of an inn or coach.

"You are most kind. But of course, I had a good teacher," she said. "He was exceptional not only as an artist but as an instructor."

I laughed. "Miss Vincy," I said, "I do not doubt that, since you tell me so. But you could give *me* the finest drawing masters in the world and I would still never be able to—"

Her mother interrupted me.

"He was *presuming*, Miss Crawley," she said sharply. "And so he was dismissed."

Rather taken aback, I murmured something in reply and the matter of Miss Vincy's tutor was dropped. I could not help but wonder if his presumption lay in attempting to engage the affections of his wealthy pupil, which would not suit the ambitions of her mother. However, Mrs. Westing began herding her company towards the card tables, and, as the stakes were reputed to be pretty high in her games, we soon found it time to go home.

I came away with a great deal of sympathy for the difficulty of Miss Vincy's position and admiration for the dignity with which she bore it, even though it was obvious that both her mother and *his* mother were determined that she should be Lord Boring's bride. The feelings of the young lady herself were more difficult to judge. True, when he spoke to her, her eyes dropped and her color rose, but this might have been due to simple self-consciousness. I could not be certain if her affections were engaged or if she was merely obedient to her mother's wishes, but in either case I pitied her.

However much the two mothers might scheme, they had not the power to bring about the marriage without the consent of the two most interested parties. Assuming that Lord Boring's income derived from his property rather than from his mother, which I had no reason to doubt, he was free to act as he wished. And all Mr. Vincy's wealth was unlikely to tempt him, as he clearly did not admire *her*. If Miss Vincy in fact had some preference for her banished tutor, that would only be yet another reason against the match. I therefore bid her good-bye with a warm smile and a pressing invitation to call at the castle.

❦ ❦ ❦

And call she did. Evidently Mrs. Westing had no objection to the Baron visiting us, so long as he had the protection of Miss Vincy's presence. Instead of the inevitable Mr. Fredericks accompanying Lord Boring and the Marquis, we now had the inevitable Miss Vincy, which in my opinion was a vast improvement.

She began my portrait, for which I sat under the pear tree in the courtyard with Fido on my lap and my embroidery at hand. I had proposed this arrangement, as I needed to be getting on with my work on the Great Hall tapestry and sitting for a portrait otherwise involved a great many hours of doing nothing in the same position every day. However, she complained that the frame was so massive that it quite hid me from view, so it had to be set to one side and I could only accomplish my mending by fits and starts.

Prudence and Charity were at first annoyed at Miss

Vincy painting my portrait, but after the first visit they ceased their complaints, discovering that they could propose a short stroll around the gardens, which Miss Vincy and I were unable to join, occupied as we were with painting and posing. Being an uncommonly determined young woman, Charity often convinced the Baron to accompany them on these strolls, from which she returned smiling and complacent.

I hoped that she was not getting her hopes raised too high. Miss Vincy, on the other hand, seemed to think that something might happen in that quarter.

"Miss Charity Winthrop enjoys the Baron's company, I believe," she said one day as we sat in dappled shade, she hard at work dabbing her brush on the canvas, I hard at work sitting still.

"Ye-es," I agreed. Certainly she enjoyed monopolizing his attention. I wasn't sure she listened to anything he said.

"She is a young lady of some fortune," Miss Vincy said.

"Yes," I agreed again.

She paused and laid down her brush for a moment, watching them as they strolled at a distance. "Who knows what may happen there?" she said, and her expression was both thoughtful and serious. I was beginning to think I was quite wrong about her tutor—even direct questioning about him and his current circumstances did not produce his name or description from the lady.

"Nothing at all, I should think," I said, rather stiffly.

Because really, it was perilously close to an insult. If Miss Vincy was going to suffer pangs of jealousy for the Baron's sake, how dare she feel them on Charity's account, with *me* sitting right in front of her?

11

THE PORTRAIT WAS NEARLY finished at last, and none too soon for me. I was beginning to grow uneasy about the Baron. Oh, not that nonsense about Charity, indulged in by Miss Vincy! That was too ridiculous to consider even for a moment.

But—Charity was certainly spending more time with him than I. I could have wished that he would have made more strenuous efforts to evade her. He might, for instance, have insisted upon remaining and reading to us; it would have been a great kindness to me, in dispelling the uncomfortable thoughts that *would* creep in during my involuntary idleness. I was beginning to fancy myself neglected and ill-treated.

I even wondered if this project, this painting of my portrait, was all an invention of Miss Vincy's to keep me away from the Baron. But no. Although Miss Vincy was more prone to spend her time with me in earnest effort than in conversation, I felt that I was beginning to know her. Such a subterfuge was beneath her.

And besides, her devotion to her work was obvious. *She* was minutely observant of every line and curve and texture of my face and figure, and I, having nothing else to occupy me, was equally observant of *her*. Frequently she lost all sense of passing time, so intent was she, and I had to ask several times for a moment's rest from my pose, because she did not hear when I spoke. Though she would not allow me, or anyone else, to see the work in progress, it was clear that her art was important to her.

I almost envied her. The world, at least the provincial, day-to-day world in which I live, does not honor those who *make* so much as those who *own*. To be a wealthy landowner of good family is to belong to the most respected class of people in England, and therefore in the world as a whole. Yet when we look back upon the past it is the artists and thinkers whose names are remembered and whose legacy is honored, not those who are merely wealthy and well-bred.

I felt a stirring of guilt, looking at Miss Vincy.

She was a good and gentle creature, as well as a talented and intelligent woman, who would make the Baron a better wife than I. Beauty is a coin squandered by time, but Miss Vincy's virtues would last throughout her life.

I was almost certain that she loved him, and had quite dismissed the tutor from my mind as a serious contender for her heart. From time to time, when she thought herself unobserved, she would allow a wistful look to steal across her face, and her hand would stray to a fine gold chain around her neck. She would withdraw a locket from her bodice which, when open, revealed a lock of hair—similar in color to His Lordship's—and press it to her lips. Perhaps after all, I thought, it would be the noble thing for me to withdraw, to give him up to her, as being the better woman.

"Miss Crawley, I pray you, think happier thoughts!" interjected Miss Vincy at this point in my musings. "You are twisting up your face like a wad of paper you are about to cast into the fire. I cannot capture the shading of your eyelid if you scowl so."

I apologized and composed my face. My mind I composed by reminding myself that Miss Vincy must, like all of us, face disappointments in life. And she was very, very rich, while I was not.

If I died an old maid, or married a man of only moderate fortune, Mama would lose her home and Alexander would lose his inheritance, not to mention our servants and perhaps our tenants being turned away. If either of these fates befell Miss Vincy, what would occur? Why nothing, save that her mother would most likely expire from spleen and disappointed ambition.

And besides, marriage would be the enemy of Miss Vincy's artistic abilities. In a short time the duties of a wife and mother would swallow up all the time and energy she now expended on her art—especially if she married a nobleman with a large estate and extensive social obligations.

Hence, it was preferable in every way that *I* should be the one to marry the Baron.

"Splendid," Miss Vincy said. "Whatever you are thinking about right now, go on thinking it. You look perfectly lovely."

So I went on thinking it, until Charity and Lord Boring returned, bringing with them Mr. Godalming.

Mr. Godalming had obviously come in order to have a look at the heiress. I imagine that he had gone calling at Gudgeon Park several times with this end in view, only to be told repeatedly that she was here, and so he had at last decided, even tho' determined to never darken our door again, to storm the castle walls in order to achieve his objective.

He evidently wished to make it clear that I was not the object of his visit, for he greeted everyone else effusively and only made one small, cold bow in my direction.

Anyone would think (I thought to myself) that he had proposed and been refused. On the contrary, I had accepted only to have him withdraw his offer.

Looking at the situation in this light, I felt much more comfortable about meeting him again in the very garden in which our interview had taken place. Why, the man was a cad! And now *he* had come to assess the possibility of wedding Miss Vincy, solely on mercenary grounds. I smiled upon him in an aloof, forgiving manner.

I could tell that Miss Vincy's appearance was a blow to him. Too wise to trust his weight to one of our tottery chairs, he perched atop the rim of a dry fountain in the center of the garden and studied her out of the corners of his eyes, heaving great, plaintive sighs like a beached whale. It never ceases to astound me how often an unattractive man like Mr. Godalming considers himself above marriage to an equally unattractive woman.

After engaging in several attempts at conversation with her as she bent her head over her work, and having those attempts rebuffed with perfect courtesy, he evidently came to the conclusion that the heiress was not to be easily gained. He shot a swift look at me and licked his red lips. I shuddered. After having had the pleasure of Lord Boring's attentions these past few months, I felt that I had had a narrow escape.

"I bring you some news," he said at last. "I had the honor to call first at Gudgeon Park, where they informed me that Mrs. Fredericks has just had notice that her son will soon be returning to our neighborhood."

Were I not still under orders to hold my pose, I should have looked at Lord Boring in surprise. He had said nothing about recalling Mr. Fredericks.

Miss Vincy looked up and stayed her brush.

"How lovely," she said softly. "I shall be so glad to see Mr. Fredericks again."

I raised my eyebrows at this response. "I did not know you were acquainted," I said. "Of course I know your father is, but I assumed it was a business relationship."

"Oh, certainly I am. Papa thinks so highly of him. He has come to dinner often at our house in London. Even Mama regards him as a sensible young man. And he is knowledgeable about painting and drawing, as well. He has said . . ." She blushed and lowered her eyes to her canvas again. "He has said kind things about my work."

Well! My gaze sharpened. I looked long and hard at Miss Vincy. Aware of my consideration, she turned away and began wiping down her brushes with a rag.

"I must not keep you any longer," she said, "Pray get up and move about. I fear you will be cramped from sitting still so long."

I smiled. How often had I pleaded in vain for a brief rest for that reason?

"When shall it be finished?" I asked, meaning the painting.

"Oh," she said, shamefaced, scanning the assembled guests to ensure no one heard this admission but me, "in truth it is done now. It is only that I prefer not to display it to so many people at once. Please, would you be so kind as to wait for a private moment before I show it to you?"

I agreed, though in truth I was burning with curiosity.

She paused in the act of lowering a cloth over the painting. "I wonder . . . I wonder what Mr. Fredericks will think of it?"

What, indeed? Ha!

I decided that I was not sorry Mr. Fredericks was returning; I had plans for his future. I would marry him off to Miss Vincy. Her gentle nature would suffer his bumptiousness without complaint, and, as unlikely as it might seem, she appeared to be at least as self-conscious when his name was mentioned as when the Baron entered the room—perhaps she could be persuaded into a *tendresse* for him. According to her, he was a man with a fine appreciation for the arts. He would understand and support her need for time away from family duties to draw and paint.

Her father admired him for some odd reason, and

even her mother, the more formidable obstacle in matters pertaining to her daughter's marriage, regarded him as "a sensible young man." Knowing the lady in question, I assumed this referred to his financial expertise. And given that expertise, he most likely had managed to save up a tidy sum, which would endear him to her even more. (How I wished that my mother were a little more like other mothers of marriageable daughters; most would make it their business to know the net worth of every single man for twenty miles round, but not my innocent mama!) And tho' the son of a man in a very humble way of life, he *was* the grandson of a baron, so with even a modest competence he would do very well for her.

He, of course, would be exceedingly lucky to get her— it would be a brilliant marriage for him as well as a suitable one. But really, his point of view was hardly worth considering.

With Miss Vincy happily married, I could wed Lord Boring without regret. When I thought of the lock of hair she carried with her and kissed in secrecy, I sighed for her disappointment. But however much she might love him, he did not return the sentiment.

No, everyone would be much better off if I arranged matters to suit myself.

"Goodness, Miss Crawley! How thankful I am that

you had not that expression on your face earlier!" cried Miss Vincy as she packed up her paints. "You quite frighten me. What *are* you planning?"

I smiled, but would not say.

❧ ❧ ❧

Mr. Fredericks returned, and all augured well for my scheme. I had not yet had the opportunity of viewing my portrait, as the rains, so common in our climate, returned in force, making visiting impossible. On the first possible day, which happened to be just after Mr. Fredericks's return, Prudence, Charity, and I walked over to Gudgeon Park.

"Miss Winthrop, how pleasant to see you again," bellowed Mr. Fredericks in a voice generally only used by herders summoning their cattle home from a distant field. "And Miss Charity Winthrop, of course! How good of you to call. And Miss Crawley. Miss *Althea* Crawley, I believe, tho' I know it is more correct to call you *Miss Crawley*, as Miss Prudence ought to be called *Miss Winthrop*." He bowed deeply and fixed me with a satirical eye, saying in a lower voice, "As you can see, I have committed all your names and the proper manner of addressing you to memory, and shall not forget again. I have not been much in company with ladies, I will confess."

He enquired after Alexander as well, and said, "Having had some leisure to consider your complaints since last we spoke, I have concluded that you were in the right. I ought to have minded Alexander more carefully, and I apologize for attempting to shift the blame onto your shoulders."

At this handsome act of contrition I blushed, remembering how I had berated him at the Screaming Stones after he had imperiled his life saving Fido's and my brother's. I realized, too, that his *appearance* as well as his *behavior* was more handsome than I had thought. He had been suffering from ill health when I first met him; now he was recovered I began to think him a very good-looking man. I resolved to exert myself to be cordial and charming.

"Thank you, sir. How *very* good to see you again," I said, dropping a curtsey. "We were quite desolated to lose your company last June. Still, I suppose the financial gentlemen in the City were the gainers for it."

He eyed me suspiciously, as tho' he had approached expecting me to fly at him like an enraged cat at a dog and now did not know what to make of my attitude. He turned to the Marquis and muttered in an audible tone, "What the devil is the woman playing at? Is that sarcasm?"

"Hush, Fredericks. The *lady* is being courteous. Answer her politely."

"I assure you, madam, the financial gentlemen in the City were *not* the gainers for being in my company in these past weeks. Quite the contrary," was Mr. Fredericks's rejoinder.

Mr. Vincy had apparently only overheard this exchange in part, for approaching us, he chuckled and said, "No, indeed, Miss Crawley! Anybody who tries to fleece Hugh Fredericks will find himself much the *loser* for it. I shouldn't like to try to bamboozle the brass out of *his* pockets, I can tell you! It would have been a joy to watch you put that pack of jackanapes in the basket, Fredericks," he continued. "Nay, miss, our Mr. Fredericks is bang up to the mark in these matters, have no fear."

From this speech I gathered that I had misjudged the nature of Mr. Fredericks's meetings with his colleagues in the City. Apparently the object of the assemblage of these merchants and men of business was to see which could best cheat the other, rather than to converse and exchange pleasantries in the civilized fashion of the landowning class.

"My apologies for underestimating him," I replied, with another curtsey.

This appeared to appease Mr. Vincy, but the look

I received from Mr. Fredericks was unexpectedly discerning.

"You think us all a vulgar lot, I perceive," he said, smiling a little. "Well, I don't say some of those fellows are not on the sharpish side." He shifted his gaze to Mr. Vincy. "How about Gentleman Jim, Vincy? Would you introduce him to your wife and daughter?"

From the horrified look Mr. Vincy gave him, I gathered that the answer was No.

"But a good many are decent folk. No less honest than the gentry, at any rate, and a great deal more so than the nobility." Here both men laughed heartily at the thought of all the deceit and double-dealing they had encountered amongst the titled classes. I was relieved that the Marquis had strolled away and was no longer a part of our little group.

Mr. Vincy was by now so at ease in the conversation that he pulled up a delicate gilt chair and sat astride it backwards, ignoring the frowns of his lady wife.

"Take Boring's mother, f'rinstance," he said in a lowered voice. "D'you know what I heard of her? She may be my hostess, but by gad, I—"

To my astonishment, Mr. Fredericks was frowning and shaking his head, either out of loyalty to his friend or—could it be?—delicacy of feeling.

Vincy flushed a dull, brick red and stood up. He bowed uneasily in my direction. "My apologies, miss. I spoke out of turn. I came up in a hard school and never have learnt to hold my tongue in polite society. I beg you'll forget I spoke." And he moved quickly away to sit at his wife's side. Evidently he assumed her proximity would have the effect of rendering him incapable of speech.

I assumed Mr. Vincy referred to Mrs. Westing's playing at cards, a practice frowned upon in some circles of the lower middle class from which he had sprung. A complete change of subject seemed to be in order.

"Miss Vincy tells me you have a keen appreciation for drawing and painting," I said to Mr. Fredericks.

He nodded, relieved to have been diverted into another theme. "I have. I started out by looking at them from a commercial aspect, you know, and after studying the subject so as to be able to put a money value on a piece, I found that they had a value for me above pounds and pence. I liked looking at them," he clarified, as though I might find this an eccentric reaction to a piece of art. "So I studied them a bit more—got to talking to artists and dealers and so on—and now I feel I understand something of the field. Not that there's not a good deal more to learn," he said, in a humbler tone than I would have expected.

He had been standing and I sitting. Now he took the little golden chair abandoned by Mr. Vincy and prepared to sit astride it as the latter had done.

"In fact, Vincy's daughter is a damned fine artist. She—"

"Mr. Fredericks!" Pleased though I was at his introducing Miss Vincy into the conversation, I could ignore neither his language nor his treatment of a fine piece of furniture. "Pray speak civilly and sit in the chair properly or not at all. You will break it."

"If it's well made I won't," he argued.

"I trust it is not part of your duties to test the workmanship of Lord Boring's carpenters by stressing the furniture to the breaking point?"

"My duties? No! But I hate to see things poorly made, cheap copies of good pieces and so on." He stood up and, upending the chair, examined its underside. "Have no fear. I recall now—I chose this set myself. Look," he thrust the chair at me so that the tips of the slender legs menaced my eyes, "see those joins? And it's solid mahogany under that gilt."

I waved the chair away and he replaced it on the floor and sat. I was pleased to see that he sat on it the right way 'round this time.

"But you were speaking of Miss Vincy," I said. "Did you know she has painted my portrait?"

His eyebrows shot up in surprise. "No, really?" he exclaimed. "I should like to see that."

I smiled on him; he was playing into my hands. "I think I can ensure that you will. I have never yet seen it myself, but I know Miss Vincy is anxious for your opinion. She does not wish to exhibit it to a large crowd for the first time. However, if I ask her nicely, she may allow you to join me in our inspection."

"Oh, pooh on asking nicely! Go and fetch her. I am quite ready."

"Mr. Fredericks—" I began, when he interrupted me.

"Do you know," he said, "you chide me without compunction when you think me thoughtless or rude. Yet you did not do so when Vincy spoke out of turn, or when he sat (as you thought) improperly on that chair. Why is that?"

I felt myself flush, but spoke casually, endeavoring to hide my confusion, "Why—why because I know you better than I know Mr. Vincy, of course!" But I did not meet his eyes and walked away quickly.

After all, I argued to myself, if I did not keep Mr. Fredericks in order, who would?

12

ONE THING BECAME CLEAR to me at the private viewing attended only by Miss Vincy, Mr. Fredericks, and myself: the portrait was something out of the common way.

In truth, it is quite difficult to judge a portrait of which you are the subject. One expects to meet the face in the mirror, but instead one sees a stranger. Yet when others were eventually allowed to see it, they cried, "Oh, what a wonderful likeness!" so I suppose I must accept the fact that this is what I look like to the rest of the world.

But beyond the likeness and the great skill with which a young woman and a dog sitting under a pear tree were depicted, something about the painting caught the eye and pulled it back again and again. When it was later exhibited to a larger audience, I noticed that, long after one would have expected people to have gazed their fill and moved on to other subjects, they stood before it in reverent silence. Sometimes they sat down and resumed their conversations only to go back for another long look.

In the social circles in which I move, the purpose of a portrait is to capture the face and figure of a sitter; nothing more. It is a private and personal item, of interest primarily to one's family and friends. However, I could tell that this painting was more important in the grand scheme of things than *I* was. My friend Miss Vincy had given me a sort of immortality. Long after we both were in our graves, this picture would be prized by people wholly unconnected to either of us, for the sake of the almost unearthly beauty it portrayed. One might expect that I would feel flattered by this, but on the contrary I was humbled.

Mr. Fredericks was actually rendered speechless by his first viewing. He looked at it for long minutes, then at the artist, shook his head in wonder and then looked back at it again.

She had been more anxious for his approbation than for mine. Her eyes were on him and not on me as she lifted the veiling cloth, which spoke volumes about the esteem in which she held him. I was beginning to suspect that all my guesses were wrong, that it was neither the dismissed tutor *nor* the Baron that she favored.

"It—it's good, isn't it?" she asked him, her voice pleading with him to tell her, yes, it was good.

He nodded. I could have shaken him for not finding voice to reassure her more fully, but she seemed satisfied. She sighed with relief, and her plain features glowed. "I know," she said, "that few women could ever be considered *great* painters, and I do not mean to put myself on a level with Miss Mary Moser or Miss Angelica Kauffmann, but I hope that this painting, with this sitter—" she suddenly seemed to recollect that the sitter was in the room, and smiled at me—"will establish me at least as a competent—"

"Oh, don't talk nonsense," Mr. Fredericks said.

Apparently unoffended by this piece of blatant rudeness, Miss Vincy turned to me and said, "I hope you will allow me to submit the picture to the Royal Academy. Mr. Fredericks, you *do* think it worthy?"

"It's worthy. Oh, they'll sky it, of course, but they'll have to show it. It's a damned fine piece of work. I'll submit it myself, if you like."

"The Royal Academy!" I exclaimed. "But, what do you mean, 'sky it'?"

Miss Vincy explained, "At the Academy exhibition hall the best-known painters' works are hung in rows at eye level, then the lesser known above that, and then the newcomers, those whose names are entirely unknown, are hung up near the ceiling—the sky, you see. Do you think that your mother would object to it being exhibited? If you wished, I could call it *Portrait of a Lady*, without identifying you by name."

"I do not think she would have any objection," I said slowly. "But . . . what about *your* mother and father? Will they allow your work to be displayed in public?"

I was very sorry to see the glow of happiness snuffed out like a candle. Her whole being appeared to droop; her gaze fell. "I do not know. But I suspect . . . I fear—"

Even Mr. Fredericks appeared somewhat crestfallen. "Old Vincy's a good sort," he said, "but he's ruled in these matters by that mutton-headed woman, your mother."

"*Mr. Fredericks!*" I protested.

Miss Vincy endeavored to hide a smile. "Really, Mr. Fredericks, I'd not think of calling my mother a *sheep*, precisely."

"Well, a rhinoceros, then, barging about and trampling people."

"*Mr.—!*"

"Oh, do hush, Miss Crawley," he said irritably, "and let me think what is to be done. It will have to be submitted anonymously: *Portrait of a Lady*, by a Lady, sort of thing. Your mother need never know."

"I couldn't go behind her back," said Miss Vincy, shaking her head.

I smiled. I knew the perfect solution to Miss Vincy's dilemma. It was not one I could propose to either at this exact moment, but it would meet all difficulties with perfect propriety.

Mr. Fredericks eyed me suspiciously. "Why do you smile, Miss Crawley? You've some idea in that head of yours, I can tell."

"No, indeed, not I!" I said. "I cannot imagine why you would think so." But I could not help smiling again.

"Oh, Mr. Fredericks," said Miss Vincy, coaxed out of her despondency by our banter, "when Miss Crawley gets that look on her face, I tremble. She is planning something, that is certain!"

And after all, I found I must just drop a hint. As we moved to join the rest of the company I said, "I suggest you both ask yourselves, what circumstances would allow Miss Vincy to exhibit the painting without fearing opposition from her parents?"

For of course, the answer to that was quite simple. If Miss Vincy were to become Mrs. Fredericks, her parents would no longer be in a position to raise any objections.

My companions turned questioning looks on me, but I would not enlighten them. Let them find out the solution themselves. With a little assistance from me, of course.

❧   ❧   ❧

My plan of action was this: now that the portrait was completed I would reclaim my rightful share of Lord Boring's attention—poor man, I would rescue him from Charity's private little tête-à-têtes—and, once Mrs. Vincy saw that the Baron would never be a match for her daughter, she would cast about for another man to wed Miss Vincy. And who better than Mr. Fredericks?

Well . . . that is to say, there might be *many* better choices, could one scour all of England, but they were not here, on the spot, and Mr. Fredericks was. And in truth, I had rather revised my opinion of Mr. Fredericks of late.

The fact that I had been unjust to him at the Screaming Stones helped to prepare my mind for the realization that everyone I loved, everyone whose opinion I valued, liked and even admired him. When I had pointed out his lack of courtesy towards the ladies of my family, he was large-minded enough to take my reproof to heart and change his ways. And when I had said that I was glad to see him again earlier, it was no more and no less than the truth. As exasperating as he was, in an odd way he stimulated and amused me. While he had been away I had felt a certain bland sameness, as though my life lacked a sprinkle of salt and a splash of lemon juice.

I was pleased to think that the friendship between the two men meant that Miss Vincy and I need not be parted, and that I would be able to assist her in keeping her wayward husband in order. Sweet natured as she was, I could not help but think she might lack the necessary decisiveness.

However, I must attend to the first item on my agenda. I searched the drawing room for Lord Boring, who was nowhere to be seen. Nor, of course, was Charity.

I said to the room as a whole, "Miss Vincy was kind enough to allow me to see my portrait first, but she begs me to let you know that now I have seen it, it is on display in the library, and anyone who will is welcome to view it."

As the group exclaimed and rose to go and see the picture, I said to Mr. Fredericks, "Perhaps you will fetch Miss Charity Winthrop and Lord Boring. I am sure they would be sorry to miss this opportunity to see it with the rest."

"Oh, I doubt it," said Mr. Fredericks. "Boring wouldn't

give two sticks for all the paintings in Somerset House. And as for that sister of yours—"

"Stepsister," I corrected. "Whether they are or are not potential patrons of the arts, I am sure they would wish to join in the entertainment of the entire party."

"Oh, very well, if you will have it so," said Mr. Fredericks in a sour tone. "I suppose you merely want Boring to come and moon over your likeness. I am going, I am going," he said hastily as he saw the look on my face, and exited the room.

It was true enough that I wanted to see Lord Boring's reaction to the portrait, and in fact it was all I could have hoped. He seemed unaware of the aesthetic and technical skills involved in its creation and appeared to regard it as a simple tribute to my beauty; as being praiseworthy only because it mirrored my face. His gaze darted between image and reality, exclaiming at their similarity.

"How grateful an artist must be," he observed to Miss Vincy, "to be presented with a subject so lovely."

"Oh, yes," said Miss Vincy. "It is truly a gift."

"Of course," said Mrs. Vincy in a sharp tone, "the subject ought to be grateful to have such a skilled painter, who can make the most of such charms as she is lucky enough to possess."

"I entirely agree," said I, trying not to laugh.

"I too," said Charity, nodding her head vigorously. "I agree with Mrs. Vincy." Charity was clearly annoyed at having her stroll with the Baron interrupted in order to view my portrait.

"In fact," said Mrs. Fredericks, attempting to make peace, "it is a perfect match: an artist whose talent is crying out for a worthy subject and a subject whose beauty is crying out to be captured on canvas. And we have reason to be grateful the two have met."

"Hmmph," said Mrs. Vincy.

"Hmmph," said Charity.

"Hmmph," said Prudence, at a rare loss for the appropriate quotation which would link my image to Eternal Night and the Great Beyond.

Everyone else, however, seemed quite pleased. "It must be framed," said Lord Boring at last. "I will ride over and have it done in York."

"No," said Mr. Fredericks. "I have arranged with Miss Vincy to take it to London."

I turned and glared at Mr. Fredericks. Why should he so officiously insist on taking it to London, when the Baron and York would do quite as well, if not better? And when had he had the time to make this arrangement with Miss Vincy? No, he had merely determined that he wished to do so for some reason.

"London!" cried Mr. Vincy. "You've only just come from London. That's a three-day ride."

"I'll allow a few weeks for the painting to dry and then I'll be off," said Mr. Fredericks.

"Look here, Fredericks," protested Lord Boring. "I'd be pleased to have it done in York. Why the long journey for a small job? And I see no reason to wait—it appears to be dry already."

"You are exhibiting your ignorance, Boring. You'd push this small miracle of a painting anyhow into your saddlebag and expect it to survive unharmed, wouldn't you? No, sorry, but the matter is settled." And Mr. Fredericks turned his back upon his employer and the head of his family and walked away.

I released a small hiss of annoyance. Mr. Fredericks, who had settled in a chair to my right, looked at me. "Yes, Miss Crawley?" he enquired.

I did not wish to explain that I had rather Lord Boring undertook the commission so that I would have occasion to consult with him about it. I therefore addressed another cause for irritation. "You were not half so solicitous about the paintings of Crooked Castle," I murmured.

His eyebrows lifted. "Ah. I see. I thought you knew. I suppose it was your father who sold the originals. They are all copies, all but the little Stubbs. I thought so when

I handled them, and the man I had up to clean them concurred."

I sat back in my chair, absorbing this blow. I had counted on being able to sell the portraits some day if the wolves began to howl too loudly at the door.

Mr. Fredericks studied me with an expression in his eyes that I was afraid might be compassion. "There is always the Stubbs," he said.

"Oh, no! I could not bear to part with that," I replied, looking down at Fido in my lap. He nodded, understanding my reason.

I thought of him saying, "I hate to see things poorly made, cheap copies of good pieces and so on," and I began to wonder. "The tapestries . . . ?"

"The one you are working on is the only one worth the effort of repairing," he said promptly. "Have you ever heard of a Jacquard loom? Ingenious invention—uses punch cards to speed up the process. Yes, they're copies, all the rest of them. Must have been done when you were a child."

I bit my lip, remembering the long-ago days when Papa was still alive. I had been too young to understand how strange it was that, though so careful about money as a general rule, he would send first the portraits and then the tapestries away to be "cleaned." And I remembered now how, when they had come back, they had looked so bright and new. They looked that way because they *were* new.

The tapestries could not be relied upon as a source of income in a pinch either. Very well.

I reverted to the original subject. "But why London?" I asked. "Could not a craftsman fit it with a frame in York as Lord Boring suggested?"

He smiled. "I have been giving some thought to your remark about the conditions under which Miss Vincy could exhibit the painting without opposition."

"Oh," I said. "And you . . . do you understand my meaning?"

"I believe I do," he replied. "Since Miss Vincy cannot bear to deceive her mother, *I* propose to do so. I will submit it to the committee as soon as it is framed."

"I see," I said, exasperated. But I could not explain, as the matter was delicate. At that moment Lord Boring called me to duplicate the pose in the painting, so that he could compare the two, and I had no opportunity to make myself clearer.

13

RELEASED FROM MY DUTIES to Art, I found the Baron almost pathetically grateful to be called away from Charity's side. The next day when Miss Vincy and the gentlemen from Gudgeon Park came to call, I chose a moment when Charity was out of the room to suggest that I was in need of a brisk walk over the moors after so much long sitting. I said that I believed Miss Vincy would likewise benefit from the same exercise. She agreed, tho' with a smile and an affectionate shake of the head—she had after all walked here from the Park only a few moments before.

Lord Boring quickly volunteered to accompany us and Mr. Fredericks followed suit. Prudence, who disliked exercise, declined to join us, as did my mother, who preferred to remain at home with Alexander. On hearing Mama's declaration, the Marquis elected to stay and keep her company. By unspoken agreement we went quickly and quietly, only slackening our pace when we had left the immediate castle grounds. I began to turn onto a path that led through a small copse of trees when the Baron said in an expressionless voice, "Ah, yes. One of Miss Charity's favorite walks."

"Oh!" I said. "You are quite right. So it is. Perhaps, as you have spent a good deal of time with my stepsister lately, you would prefer to try something different? The cliff walk for instance? I know Charity dislikes it—it is rather windy."

"By all means!" agreed the Baron. Then, remembering his manners, he added, "If it is agreeable to you, Miss Vincy, that is."

Miss Vincy said that she would be pleased to walk the cliffs, as she had never done so before, and we soon gained the path that led towards the sea. Her artist's eye was delighted with the sun glittering on the placid sea far below and the vast panorama laid out before us. The wind, however, was powerful enough to necessitate our each taking a gentleman's arm to steady us, and I called Fido back to me, away from the edge. I took care to secure the Baron's arm and, as the other two proceeded ahead of us, I was pleased to note how happy she seemed, pointing out details of the scene below. She looked quite attractive, with the wind in her hair and her color high.

The Baron said, "You have grown fond of Miss Vincy, I think?"

I turned to him. "Oh I have! Very fond."

"Yes, she seems genteel enough—surprising, really, given the father. 'Tis a pity about the smallpox," he mused. "Without the scars she might have been tolerable-looking, but with them—!"

"Oh, but there is so much more to Miss Vincy than her looks or her parentage," I cried, feeling a prick of annoyance on my friend's account. "Fie, Lord Boring! Do not make me think that you see so little below the surface!"

I was not smiling as I said it and he reddened. "I beg your pardon. I was only thinking that few men will want to marry her save for her fortune. We men, you know, are more apt to be beguiled by a lovely face than a worthy nature."

"Only to discover your mistake," I retorted, "after the first six months of marriage."

He laughed. "Oh I doubt many men who marry for love look past the first six months."

"Then, Baron, men are greater fools than I thought." I said this with a good deal of vigor, and Lord Boring looked a little taken aback. I could not repent of it, however.

"Of course," he said after a brief silence, "some young

ladies combine great beauty with great good nature," and he smiled, with the clear intention of paying me a compliment.

"Oh?" I enquired testily. "They may be rarer than you think."

We walked for a time without speaking, during which I mentally shook myself all over and came to my senses. What was the matter with me? I had always known, ever since I was thirteen years old and men first began to look at me, that beauty was power, the only real power (other than cash in hand) that a woman could possess. I knew it was transitory, and must be used shrewdly and well in the few years it lasted.

It had seemed the natural order of things. And I was one of the lucky ones. Why should I question it?

"I beg your pardon, Lord Boring," I said. "That was rude. Sometimes it is difficult to be a woman."

He rallied at my apology, responding, "Oh, but Miss Crawley, lovely as you are, surely *you* of all ladies cannot find being a woman to be a burden!"

Ah well. He was charming, handsome, wealthy, and titled. I supposed it was a bit much to expect him not to be a fool like the rest of his sex.

❦ ❦ ❦

Having reestablished Lord Boring as my admirer and broken the seeming stranglehold my stepsister had had upon his company (for now that my posing sessions were completed, he reverted to his former habits, joining me as we sat or walked or rode), I turned my attention to other matters. I must find a way to spur Mr. Fredericks on to propose to Miss Vincy. I decided that, as Mr. Godalming continued to call at the castle and the Park, staring morosely at Miss Vincy and making occasional attempts to converse with her, I might as well make use of him.

Perhaps this was wrong of me, but I could not quite forgive Mr. Godalming for first abusing me for being mercenary and then pursuing Miss Vincy with the identical motivation. Especially as he was quite wealthy already and did not need the money; it was nothing but greed. This being the case I engaged him in conversation when next I spotted him in the village. He was in Sturridge's shop, frowning over the purchase of a handkerchief.

"Choose the linen, Mr. Godalming," I recommended, coming up behind him. "It will stand up to washing better than the silk."

He bowed and said in a lofty tone, "How do you do, Miss Crawley? I thank you for your advice, but I believe I am as good a judge of handkerchiefs as any young lady," and proceeded to purchase the silk. Ah well. No one could say I hadn't warned him—it was a cheap silk and would fade badly.

The subject matter, however, gave me an idea. "Speaking of handkerchiefs," I went on, "as we are such old friends, I hope you will not mind my saying that I think you were blind to the signals a certain young lady was sending you, only the other day."

He paused in the act of pocketing the new handkerchief. "Oh?" he said, his nose twitching like a rabbit's. He licked his lips. "And which young lady was that?"

"No, no, Mr. Godalming, you must not ask me that! I only wished to drop a hint. You have heard of the language of handkerchiefs now so popular in London and Bath?"

"I—I believe so."

In truth, I myself had only recently heard of it from the Marquis, whose information had not been complete enough to tell me the details of what each gesture meant, so it was necessary for me to fabricate. However, this was of no importance, as Mr. Godalming, who had hardly ever left his home county, would be none the wiser, and I doubted that the practical and levelheaded Miss Vincy, who *did* move in fashionable society, had ever bothered her head with such a silly means of conducting a flirtation.

"For instance, when a refined young lady wishes a gentleman to know that she would enjoy entertaining his attentions, she glances at him and then brushes her right cheek with her handkerchief."

"Is that so? Indeed, I did not know. I thank you for telling me. I shall be alert in the future."

"The glance may be brief," I cautioned him. "A lady cannot be too obvious, you understand."

"Oh, certainly. Indeed!"

After this conversation, it was a simple matter to achieve my goal. It only required that Miss Vincy, Mr. Godalming, Mr. Fredericks, and I be in company together.

"Miss Vincy," I said as we stood in the hallway of Gudgeon Park, "I beg you will look at Mr. Godalming's cravat and tell me if it is not tied in the style of the Prince Regent's friend, Beau Brummell."

Miss Vincy laughed and disclaimed any knowledge of how this famous dandy arranged his neckwear, but she looked as I had directed.

"Oh!" I said, "you have a black smudge on your cheek. The right one."

Ever obliging, Miss Vincy raised a lace-trimmed handkerchief and scrubbed her cheek with it, perhaps a bit more vigorously than would be appropriate for a seductive signal. "Is it gone?"

"Almost," I said, "a bit more to the side . . . gently! You will take your skin off." I continued, "But you have not given me your opinion of Mr. Godalming's cravat."

She paused with her handkerchief to her cheek and looked again.

"What do you think?" I asked.

She dropped her eyes. "Hush, Miss Crawley. He is looking at us."

Mr. Godalming *was* looking at us, thank goodness. Smiling broadly, he joined us within the twinkling of an eye. I raised my eyebrows and nodded by way of encouragement.

"Miss Vincy and I were discussing whether or not your valet receives his inspiration for your cravat from the fashions of the Royal Court." I doubted whether Mr. Godalming's valet had any conception that there was more than one way to tie a neck cloth.

Mr. Godalming, however, had no misgivings on the subject. "Why yes, I believe you are correct. Williams is very anxious that his young master should look as dashing as possible, even living in the country as we do." Here he giggled and bowed to Miss Vincy, who cast an imploring look in my direction. I hardened my heart. This was for her own good, whether she knew it or not.

"I hope you will excuse me," I said. "I must speak to

Mr. Fredericks for a moment." I smiled sweetly at Miss Vincy and pried her detaining hand off my wrist. "I will be only a moment," I assured her.

"But—"

She watched me go with despairing eyes, then resigned herself, allowing Mr. Godalming to find her a secluded seat where he could have her to himself. When I reached Mr. Fredericks I looked back. Her eyes were lowered to her clasped hands in her lap, while Mr. Godalming had draped his bulk over a nearby chair in a masterful attitude and was holding forth on some subject. Recollecting his courtship of me, I suspected it would be something about the cultivation of turnips. Either that or the treatment of liver flukes in sheep.

Mr. Fredericks had the appearance of passing through the room on his way elsewhere. I nearly had to clutch at his sleeve to halt his forward progress. He had a pen in one hand and some papers in the other; evidently he was engaged in some business. He stopped and regarded me with a sardonic light in his eyes.

"Well, Miss Crawley? Did you waylay me in order to lecture me on my manners? If so, I must beg off—I've a great deal of work in hand."

"No, certainly not. Have you been using the tails of

your jacket as a pen-wiper again? I cannot believe the Baron has no blotting paper or old rags which would better suit the purpose. However, that is not what I wished to speak to you about." I steered him to a quiet corner ideally suited for my purposes. We had an excellent view of the preening, gesticulating Mr. Godalming and only a partial one of the shrinking, reluctant Miss Vincy.

"It is Miss Vincy I wished to speak of. I believe that we are both her good friends?"

"*I* certainly am. As for you, Miss Crawley . . ." He broke off. "Well yes, I dare say you are," he conceded. "She has not had many friends, of either sex. I am glad she has you."

Touched by this unexpected tribute, I spoke with real emotion. "Then I hope you will believe me that anything I do or say about her is with her best interests in mind."

He considered this. "Perhaps in *your* mind, that is so. But you are an interfering young woman, and I don't trust you in the least when you are in this mood."

"The only mood I am in," I said, annoyed, "is one of deep concern for Miss Vincy's future. Look at her," I commanded. Mr. Fredericks sighed, but looked.

"I have spoken to Mr. Godalming. I cannot say that he confided in me entirely," I said truthfully, "but he gave me the distinct impression that he was determined to woo and win her. And I am certain that he is so determined, not out of any appreciation for the qualities that you and I value in her, but rather for the fortune that will come with her."

Mr. Fredericks was silent, watching as Mr. Godalming puffed out his chest and laughed.

"Mr. Godalming is not the man of delicacy or sensitivity either of us could wish to see become her husband. He would not care or understand about her feelings for her artistic work. He would expect her to produce an heir and supervise his household—that is all. He would not love or esteem her."

"Well, what of it?" he said. "Let him propose. She's no fool. She'll not have him."

I looked at him steadily. "Her mother is determined to see her married. If not to the Baron—and I have good reasons to think him indifferent to her if not actually averse—then to some other man, preferably one of whom she approves, in a respectable position in life. And you will have observed as well as I have that she is an obedient and dutiful daughter. Much more so, I will own, than *I* would be in her situation."

"Oh *you*! I've no doubt of that! You'd run rings around that detestable woman."

I arched an eyebrow. "Yes, I probably would, though you ought not to say it, either *of* her or *to* me."

He waved this away as being of no importance. "And what, pray, do you expect me to do about this situation?"

Here I was forced to prevaricate a little. What I wanted, of course, was for him to marry her himself, but I could not say so. My gaze dropped and I shook my head.

"I do not know. Perhaps you could talk to her? She thinks so highly of you, and values your opinion so. I have spoken of Mr. Godalming to her, but my words seem to have made little impression on her." Strictly speaking, this was true. "You have known her longer than I, and she will accept your estimate of another man."

"What! I am to undertake delicate subjects of conversation with a young lady? I thought it was your belief that I was a blundering oaf without an ounce of tact in my body."

I smiled. "You are not tactful, Mr. Fredericks, I agree. But I believe that where you care for someone you will be a staunch and true friend. Sometimes a little blunt honesty from someone who cares for us is what we most need. And . . . and you are not an oaf. Rather the contrary, I am beginning to think."

He mulled this over in silence for a time. Then he stood up and said gruffly, "If I see any sign she is likely to yield to Godalming's blandishments, I'll talk to her. But I expect this is really all a plot to clear the field so that *you* can spread your nets to catch Boring for yourself." Then he strode out of the room, leaving me tapping the toe of my shoe in irritation.

14

NOW THAT MR. GODALMING believed he had received a signal that encouraged him to press his suit, he ignored any genuine signals Miss Vincy sent in his direction. Her downcast face when he spoke to her, her turning away when he approached, even her abruptly leaving a room as he entered it—all these he attributed to shyness, to shame at her own boldness in having beckoned him to her side.

In the next few weeks he called on her every day. If he could not find her at the Park, he followed her to the castle. If, in an attempt to avoid him, she went out walking or riding, he went walking or riding as well, until he had caught her up.

Almost I repented of my interference in her affairs when I saw how distressed she was by his blind, unrelenting pursuit. *Almost.* For Mr. Fredericks also observed her distress. He saw Mr. Godalming herding his quarry into the conservatory, like one of his tenants' sheepdogs harrying a ewe into a shearing pen. He watched as Mr. Godalming fussily adjusted a pillow for her back and fetched cups of tea and biscuits, insisting that she eat and drink when she did not want to. And as Mr. Fredericks watched, his brow knitted and his face darkened.

But still he did not declare himself.

One day when she was at the castle and Mr. Godalming had been circling her like an annoying gnat at a picnic, she broke away from him and, slipping her arm into mine, pulled me out of the room.

"Please, Miss Crawley," she said in a low, urgent voice, "may we not go, perhaps"—she paused, evidently trying to think of somewhere Mr. Godalming could not follow—"to your bedchamber?"

"Yes of course, my dear," I said, feeling guilty for my part in this persecution. "And if you wish, I can say that you were taken ill and must lie down for a while. He will have to go home *some*time."

"No," she said. "If I did that, he would tell my parents and they would call the doctor. I am rarely ill."

She sank down on a chair near the window and, as the daylight fell on her face I was shocked at how haggard she appeared.

"Oh, my dear Miss Vincy," I cried, repentant, "he will

have to propose soon, and then you can turn him down. All this will be at an end."

She was silent and her head drooped. "Don't you see?" I persisted. "When you give him your refusal, he will go and with any luck you will never see him again."

She passed her hand across her face, and I realized her eyes were reddened, as if with weeping. Surely a persistent suitor alone could not have reduced her to such a state.

"Miss Vincy, what is it? Please believe that I am your friend. I would give anything—" I thought of the Baron and amended—"*almost* anything to make you happy."

She smiled, and a single tear coursed down her cheek and was dashed away. "I know that you are my friend. Please believe *me* that I value your affection."

"Then tell me why you do not send the odious Mr. Godalming about his business."

"I cannot," she said. "If he does propose, I must accept. My mother—"

"*What?* Oh Miss Vincy! It is all very well to be a dutiful daughter, but really, there *are* limits! Englishwomen of the nineteenth century are not cattle, not possessions to be bartered off to the first comer! Well," I said, reconsidering this rash statement, "perhaps they are in a *certain* sense, but not literally so. Your parents may be disappointed at a refusal and therefore they may say bitter things to you. Legally," I admitted, "they might also be entitled to lock you up in your room or even cast you out to fend for yourself clad only in your shift, yes, that is true. But in *law* they cannot force you to wed against your will. Unless, of course," I mused, "they have bribed the parson, in which case—"

"You do not understand," said Miss Vincy. "I have given my solemn word of honor that if a gentleman of good name and fortune offers for me, I will accept. Oh, my mother would prefer the Baron for me, of course, or any other member of the aristocracy, but she knows that it will not—that he does not—In short, she has nearly lost hope on that account." She kept her eyes low, not meeting mine.

"But *why*? Why would you give such an undertaking, Miss Vincy?"

Once again she rubbed at her eyes. She shook her head. "You do not understand. And I cannot tell you. No, my only hope is that some miracle occurs and he does not ask. And Mr. Godalming is the least of my miseries."

I stared at her, stricken. What had I done?

I supposed that what she meant by Mr. Godalming being the least of her worries was that she had lost the

Baron as well, which did not make me like myself any better. As I sat holding her hand, berating myself for my foolish meddling, I began to feel a certain irritation. Not with Miss Vincy, of course, but with Mr. Fredericks. Why on earth had he not done as I had intended him to, and made an offer for her himself? Really, he was the most aggravating man! He called himself her friend, he clearly admired her and enjoyed her company, and yet he would not do this simple thing to save her from a life of wretchedness as Mrs. Godalming.

Well, I would go and tell him what I thought of him.

"Miss Vincy," I said, "lie down upon the bed and I will fetch you a glass of wine to help you compose yourself."

"But—"

"I will say you are well save for a small headache. And I will send Mr. Godalming away."

It was this last promise, I think, that made her obedient to my command. Without another word she climbed onto the bed and leaned back against the pillows.

Downstairs I looked about for Mr. Godalming, determined to be rid of him as soon as possible. He was nowhere in sight. I whirled about, straining to see if he had got past me and crept up the stairs. I should not have been surprised to discover him even now tapping doggedly at my bedroom door, determined not to allow Miss Vincy one moment of privacy until she agreed to become his wife.

He was so absolutely not present that I began to fear that the boards of the trapdoor to our oubliette (a faithful copy of the secret prison into which the kings of old were wont to drop their enemies) had given way underneath his weight—lord knows they were rotten enough.

The only gentleman in view was Mr. Fredericks, and I advanced upon him with the light of battle in my eyes.

He regarded me with a quizzical smile. "Ah! I see that Zeus' warrior maid, gray-eyed Athena, approaches, and she is in the devil of a temper. Is something the matter, Miss Crawley?"

"Althea, not Athena," I snapped, although I knew full well that he was making a reference to the Greek goddess, which, now I thought of it, was not what one would expect from the son of a shopkeeper. "Yes, there is something the matter!"

"Perhaps you are still concerned about the way that Mr. Godalming has been doting on Miss Vincy, to her obvious discomfort?"

"Yes, I am." I subjected him to a hard stare. He was barely managing to hide a self-satisfied smile.

"I think you will find that Mr. Godalming is no longer a matter of concern." He lowered his eyes in mock modesty, affecting to flick an invisible mote of dust off a grubby sleeve.

"How so, Mr. Fredericks?" Surely not the oubliette?

"Inexplicably, Mr. Godalming has got the idea that old Vincy is fast approaching dun territory." At my mystified look, he further explained, "Purse-pinched, Miss Crawley, on the rocks, dished, at low ebb. In short, Mr. Godalming believes that Mr. Vincy hasn't a sixpence to scratch himself with. Naturally, being the sort of man he is, he promptly made himself scarce."

"Oh, but—no one would believe *that!* Look at their coach, their servants, their garb! Why Mrs. Vincy's dresses alone—!"

Mr. Fredericks looked amused. "My dear Miss Crawley! I had no idea you knew so little of the world. Why, I could name fine gentlemen, and ladies, too, not twenty miles from here who haven't a feather to fly with, but who nevertheless put on a brave show. There are all sorts of ways to look as though you are flush with funds when in fact you've scarcely enough in your pockets to jingle as you walk. It wouldn't do, you see, for a man like Vincy to look poor. His lady, his daughter, his servants and equipage must be superbly got up, with everything bright and shining about them, or, you see, investors will lose confidence in him."

"Then . . . then you mean . . . it is true?" I asked, aghast.

"Oh, Lord no. Vincy is a sly dog. He's had some close calls over the years, of course, but you wouldn't see him letting Mrs. Vincy go out in public in a cheap frock when times were thin. Not that *she'd* stand for it for one moment, anyway, even though she brought nothing to the marriage but her name and lineage."

"I see," I said, much relieved.

"Godalming was worried he'd compromised himself, given the amount of attention he'd paid to Miss Vincy. Which, if she thought him anything other than a nuisance, would be quite true. And of course the old lady thinks she's got him roped and tied."

I opened my mouth to berate him for referring to a gentlewoman in Mrs. Vincy's position as "the old lady," but he forestalled me.

"Oh, you know perfectly well that you don't like her either. In any case, I advised him to invent urgent business calling him to York. Then he can lay low until they leave."

"Until they leave! But this is high summer. Mr. Godalming has an estate which must be attended to. I thought— I had hoped that they would stay many months longer."

He shook his head. "Not now. Since Mrs. Vincy has lost all hopes of catching the Baron," here he regarded me with what I can only describe as a baleful gaze, "and the only other local marital possibilities for her daughter are now exhausted," here he looked at me again, "they will leave soon. She will wait a few weeks, both for decorum's sake, and to make sure Godalming will not return, but leave she will, and soon."

"I see," I said, and left him.

So immense was my sense of guilt that I brought Miss Vincy an entire glass of wine unadulterated by water, some of the last of the great wine cellar. I longed to beg her pardon, but I could not bear to admit how greatly I had been at fault.

I eased the door open gently, fearing she might be asleep, and found her bent, unconscious of my intrusion, over a letter. At first she read the letter and then she kissed the locket with the twist of hair which depended from her neck.

"Oh, my dearest, my darling," she murmured.

I stamped my feet a few times to ensure she knew of my presence.

"Oh, Miss Crawley! I did not hear—is Mr. Godalming gone?" She slipped the letter back into her pocket and the locket back into the neckline of her dress.

"He is," I said, handing her the goblet. "I do not believe he will cause you any further trouble. Mr. Fredericks has spoken to him." I thought it best not to mention exactly *how* he had dissuaded Mr. Godalming from annoying her further.

"Bless him! Mr. Fredericks is such a good friend, much better than I deserve."

"Nonsense," I said briskly, thinking of Mr. Fredericks's failure to propose. "You deserve far better, but we must do our best with the materials at hand."

"Miss Crawley," she said, laughing a little, "you are most unkind to Mr. Fredericks! He admires you greatly, you know."

"Pooh! Nothing of the kind! He is as rude as possible to me, and never fails to point out my faults, which, according to him, are legion."

"But you do the same to him, you know you do! Indeed, I think you two are much alike. We live in an age of manners, when it is accounted a virtue never to speak plain. But you and Mr. Fredericks pay no mind to such conventions; you say what you think."

My jaw dropped open. I knew I had a ready tongue, but *really!* "I? I am as rude as Mr. Fredericks? *I?*"

The tears in her eyes had receded and she was laughing. "Do you know, Miss Crawley, if I had suggested the same thing to Mr. Fredericks—that you are alike in that way—I believe he would have responded in exactly the same way, both in phrasing and intonation."

At least I had gotten her to forget her troubles enough to laugh, and I thought it worth it, even at the expense of being the object of her laughter.

15

"A BOLT FROM THE BLUE." I have sometimes read of an unexpected event described in this way, and now I know exactly what is meant by the phrase.

A blue sky, a sunny, mild day. The usual list of worries and troubles runs through one's mind, but nothing that cannot be overcome, nothing that will not reach a satisfactory conclusion eventually, if not today, why then, tomorrow. An ordinary day, in fact. And then lightning strikes from out of that innocent blue sky and all that remains is the smoking ruins of one's every hope and every dream.

Busy with my household duties, I allowed Charity to snare Lord Boring and take him off for a stroll about the grounds. I had become resigned to the fact that I could not trust him to refuse her overtures when I was not available, and Mama and I had a great inventory of linens before us that morning. How was I to know the danger? How could I have guessed?

They were gone for a long time: several hours, in fact. Mama and I concluded, correctly, as it happened, that they had gone to the Park. At last they returned.

"Boring, go and speak with Stepmama," Charity ordered as soon as they were within doors, and Lord Boring obeyed.

"Mrs. Winthrop, may I have a word with you in private?" he said, avoiding my gaze.

"Why certainly," Mama said, looking a bit surprised. They retired to the little boudoir near the dining hall, leaving a startled silence behind.

Or at least, a startled silence on my part. Charity sat down and clasped her hands in her lap, with a smug look on her face. Prudence knew that something of great moment was in the air. She cast enquiring glances at Charity, which Charity ignored.

At last, unable to bear the suspense, Prudence said coyly, "And so, dear sister, have you any *news* you wish to tell us?"

"Thank you, Prudence," Charity replied, "but I think it best if we wait for Stepmama." Both sisters darted sudden looks in my direction, which were immediately withdrawn.

After an interval of some ten minutes Lord Boring came out. Mama stood in the doorway, her face white, her dark eyes meeting mine with an expression I could not interpret.

"Charity," she said, "come here, please."

Charity rose and followed her into the boudoir. As she did so, Lord Boring said, "I—you won't want me any further, will you? For the moment, I mean? My mother wished me to return."

"Very well, Boring," Charity said, "you must go to your mother. We will see you tomorrow morning, however."

"Yes, yes of course. Till the morning, then." He bowed, smiled uneasily upon Prudence and me and made his escape.

Charity was with Mama for an even shorter period of time. When she came out, Mama beckoned to me. When I joined her in the boudoir, she, like everyone else for the past twenty minutes, avoided meeting my eyes.

"Sit down, Althea, dear. I—that is, Charity and Lord Boring have some news which I should like to break to you—or rather, not break to you, only tell you—in private. She—they plan to marry. Lord Boring proposed this afternoon and she accepted."

"Charity and . . . Lord Boring?" My mother nodded. "They plan to marry?" She nodded once again, looking at me anxiously. I shook my head at her. "Oh, Mama, you cannot be serious! Did Charity tell you so?"

"Lord Boring told me so first, Althea. Charity confirmed it, as I also was incredulous. After so many months of marked attentions to you, to turn around and propose to Charity! I could scarcely believe it. And yet, my dearest"—here she rose and put her arms around me—"it *is* true. His mother knows and approves of the match. Indeed, I suspect it was her idea. He does not behave like an ardent lover whose proposal has been accepted. I believe he will marry her out of respect for his mother's wishes, rather than his own."

How could it be? Yet another submissive child, willing to sacrifice her or his life's happiness on the altar of filial duty!

"But *why*? I fully understand that Charity would have him if she could, but why should he want her? And why should his mother wish to see them marry?"

My mother lowered her gaze and her voice. "I believe it may be Charity's fortune that is behind it," she murmured. "And of course, Charity is quite a pretty girl. Nothing in comparison with you, of course, but attractive."

"But Lord Boring already has a fortune. And he doesn't *like* Charity." My voice was rising into a wail, and I stilled it by pressing a hand to my mouth.

"Now, dear, let us hope you are wrong. When she is

in a good mood, she can be pleasant enough. No, but I fear it *is* financial necessity that prompted his proposal. The Marquis has several times hinted to me that the Baron was unlikely to offer for you, because you have no dowry. I have been fretting a great deal about whether or not to mention it to you. It seemed so obvious that he was very taken with you, and you seemed . . ." Her voice trailed off.

"Very taken with him," I concluded for her. "Yes. Yes, I was."

"But Althea, dear, I have never thought you to be *in love* with him. Attracted, yes, of course you were—he is such a handsome man and his manners are faultless. But he does not seem to me to be a man of strong character. He seems—forgive me, dear—rather weak. And you have such a decided character that I would wish you to marry a man who was your equal.

"To be honest," she continued, "I am even a bit concerned about his marrying Charity. The Marquis also suggested that the Boring fortune is much smaller than we have supposed and that Mrs. Westing has . . . gambling debts. Debts of a serious nature, that she is not in a position to pay. I worry that this marriage may not be in Charity's best interests. I ventured to say so—not so bluntly as that, of course, but urging her to consider her position before entering into a formal engagement. She—

she accused me of seeking to keep her money in the family for my own selfish purposes. After that, of course, I could say nothing else."

I reflected that it was quite true that we wished to keep her money in the family. We could not deny it. But since she kept such a tight grip on every penny, it was only *just* worth the effort. I did not envy the Baron if he thought he would have free access to it for his own purposes. He might have every legal right to it once they were married, but Charity was a force to be reckoned with in these matters.

Nor did I envy Charity. She would be married for her fortune and, I supposed, because she was prettier than (tho' not so rich as) Miss Vincy. I knew beyond a doubt that, given a free choice, he would have married me, and Charity knew it as well.

"Charity will be a baroness," I said aloud. "And I suppose that is all that matters."

"Perhaps. But it is wrong for me to assume the match is not based upon affection. At any rate, we must hope so. My greatest fear is how it concerns you, my love. Please tell me that you are not so very unhappy."

I considered my emotions. The honest truth was that I was both angry and offended. My vanity was injured. But my heart . . . my heart was untouched. Mama was right. I did not love him. I had merely marked him out as my property, and now was furious that I had lost him, and to *Charity*.

At last I spoke. "He was wrong to have distinguished me with so much attention if he did not mean to marry me. That has lessened him in my eyes to such an extent that I am not sorry I am not to be his wife. I am distressed, yes, but I will recover in time."

"Oh, how grateful I am to hear you say so!" said my mama, pressing her hand to her heart. "I have been so frightened! But as you remarked only this spring, you are young yet at seventeen. Many years lie ahead in which you will have the opportunity to meet the man who will make you a good husband and father to your children."

A thought struck me, and I smiled.

"I believe I am growing too refined in my taste, Mama. Last spring I thought I would be glad to marry anyone, so long as he had the wherewithal to save the castle. I agreed to marry *Mr. Godalming*. The only thing that saved me from that fate was his chagrin at discovering my motive. Now listen to me! I regard a handsome nobleman as not good enough for me! I demand to marry a man I both like and respect!" And I shook my head at my own folly.

"Liking and respecting one's husband, even loving him wholeheartedly all your lives together, is possible," Mama said. "Your papa was a fine man. Had it not been for my love of you, and concern for my unborn child, I believe I would have died of grief at his death."

"Yes," I said. "I know. I remember."

"The sole reason I married Mr. Winthrop so soon was—"

"I know, Mama. I know. You tried to do the best you could for your children. I understood then and I understand now. You have no need to explain."

"Good. But you must marry a fine man, too, whatever the financial consequences may be. I could not bear to see you unhappy."

"Very well, I shall try. Do you know, Mama? I believe this situation has a positive side. With Charity married off, we shall have one less mouth to feed!"

❧   ❧   ❧

I tried to keep this aspect of the state of affairs in mind as we rejoined my stepsisters. Imagine, I told myself as I went to Charity and embraced her, imagine not having to endure her petty jealousy every day, not having to allow her precedence every time we walked down a hall together. Imagine, I thought as I congratulated her on her upcoming nuptials, not having to listen to her shrill rendition of "The Bluebells of Scotland" of an evening, or being able to give Alexander a sweet without fearing that Charity would filch it as soon as my back was turned.

"How grand it will be to have a baroness for a sister, will it not, Prudence?" I said, gaining strength from the deflated expressions on their faces. They had both expected me to be crushed by the news. Well, I *was* crushed, to a degree. But I was able to remain with them for a good quarter of an hour, discussing the match in measured tones, before I made an excuse and left them.

Fido and I climbed the stairs to my bed chamber, and I curled up in my bed with my dog (the dog that *he* had given me!) and had a little weep.

After a time I began to think of my friend Miss Vincy. She too had lost the Baron by means of this day's events. Perhaps she had had less cause for hope than I had, but the heart is not always reasonable in these matters. I remembered the letter I had seen her reading. Could it have been a letter from the Baron explaining his intentions? If so, it was more explanation than *I* had received. I decided that, on the morrow when the Baron came calling, I would remain at home long enough to grant him civil good wishes on his engagement, and then go and seek out Miss Vincy.

❧   ❧   ❧

"Ah, Miss Crawley. Good morning."

As it happened, I was the only one downstairs when the Baron arrived. Judging by the expression on his face, he had hoped to arrive early enough to whisk his fiancée out-of-doors without encountering me at all. He would realize soon enough that his lady love was not an early riser.

I allowed a small pause to occur before responding, and searched his handsome face and form for some telltale little sign I ought to have seen that would have alerted me to the fact that he was a weak-willed, despicable, mercenary . . .

Of course, *I* had been prepared to wed for money, myself.

I sighed, went to him, and shook him by the hand. "Welcome to the family, my lord," I said. "Many congratulations on your engagement."

"I—I thank you for your generous words," he stammered. "You were—I suppose you were surprised to hear of it?"

"I was," I acknowledged, "but this is the last time we should speak of it. You are to wed Charity, which means we will be brother and sister. I would not wish to be at odds with such a close relative."

He bent forward to say in a lower tone, "I beg of you to believe me that I wished to address you, to ask you to do me the honor of becoming my wife. If I had had the freedom of choice! Then you may be certain—"

"Please," I said. "Say no more about it. It is in the past, and you must look to the future."

He scowled at this reminder. "Well do I know it. Fear not, I will pay for having courted you more assiduously than I did Charity. *She* would not have been so kind as you have just been. I know the character of the woman I will wed."

In fact, I doubted this, but he would learn.

I reflected that had he married for attraction alone he could have had me. Had he married for money alone, he could have had Miss Vincy. Instead he had chosen a compromise between the two and had ended up with Miss Charity Winthrop.

I did not think he could have done worse for himself if he'd tried.

16

WALKING FROM CROOKED CASTLE to Gudgeon
Park on a fine day when there is no fear of soiling one's
stockings, it is faster and more pleasant to use the foot-
path across Farmer Macomb's land rather than the high
road. One therefore approaches Gudgeon Park from the
rear instead of the front.

It was thus that I witnessed Mr. Fredericks assist-
ing a heavily veiled lady to climb a stile over a fence in a
surreptitious manner. That is to say, Mr. Fredericks was
behaving in a calm and collected way, but the lady cast
hunted looks over her shoulder as though pursued by
footpads or murderers. Although I could not see her face,
I had little doubt of her identity. Shrouding her head and
shoulders was the fine lace shawl Miss Vincy had been
wearing on our first acquaintance, and unless her maid
had chosen this moment to make off with both Mr. Fredericks *and* her mistress's lace mantilla, I could not help
but feel that this was the lady herself.

That this was an elopement seemed obvious. Not only the haste and secrecy of this back-door exit from the Park grounds convinced me, but the fact that Mr. Fredericks was carrying a bulging satchel, no doubt filled with clothing and other oddments thought necessary for their flight.

Well!

As the stile Mr. Fredericks and Miss Vincy were negotiating led to a path in full view of the one on which I stood, I hastily retreated to a little wood some hundred feet away where I would not be seen. I picked Fido up in my arms and slipped behind a massive old oak to watch them as they passed.

I could not hear what they said to one another, beyond that the lady asked several anxious questions, which were answered by the gentleman in a reassuring tone. *She* was agitated, while *he* was soothing.

Perhaps you think it wrong that I should spy on them in this way, but I was not equal to pursuing any other course at the moment. At the sight of these two stealing off together, I felt as though I had been kicked in the midsection by a draft horse. I clutched my dog so tightly that he whined and looked up at me. I kissed his forehead in apology and loosened my grip, bracing myself against the possibility that I might scream or fall upon the ground.

It would have been quite reasonable to have felt a great deal of curiosity at this method of beginning a new life together—why should Mr. Fredericks not have applied to his old friend Mr. Vincy for permission to marry his daughter in the usual way?—but any interest I might have felt in this question was swamped by another, different sensation.

I was furious.

The pain and anger that had swept across me at Lord Boring's defection were as nothing compared with my feelings now. For months I had plotted and schemed to marry the Baron. And for months Mr. Fredericks had annoyed and exasperated me beyond measure. Even in recent weeks when I had come almost to like the man, I had had no feelings for him beyond friendship. Nor had he given any indication of an interest in me. I had *wanted* him to marry Miss Vincy, for heaven's sake!

So why, since the Baron was to marry Charity and Mr. Fredericks apparently to marry Miss Vincy, was I far more upset by the latter than the former?

Lord Boring was a shallow, weak man, no better than a cut-out paper doll. A few sighs, a tear or two, and I had done with grieving for his loss. But Mr. Fredericks . . .

I once had believed his Lordship to be all that was noble, cultivated, and worthy and Mr. Fredericks to be an ignorant, ill-mannered, pestilent boor. My opinions were now reversed. It was *Mr. Fredericks* who was the man of culture and character, not the Baron.

And I also realized that I no longer wished him to marry Miss Vincy. In fact, I wished she would remove her hand from his arm. At once. I stared after the runaway couple with narrowed eyes and heaving breast. How *could* they? Without even *discussing* it with me?

In order not to have to dwell upon the irrationality of my mental and emotional state, I put Fido down and began to follow them. This was not easy to do unobserved, as the path they took led over a treeless field which was inhabited by a flock of sheep. I supposed that they were taking this less conspicuous route to the village of Lesser Hoo, where they might engage a coach to take them to York or perhaps even Gretna Green in Scotland, so they could be married immediately. I went after them, but kept to the woods along the edge of the field, to avoid being detected. This entailed a great deal of stumbling over logs, twisting my ankle as I stepped on loose rocks that shifted under my weight, and being slapped across the face by tree branches. My muffled squeaks of irritation and pain so unnerved Fido that he barked in alarm.

"Oh, hush!" I ducked behind a tree as the others turned their heads in our direction.

Interested by the small commotion in one corner of their pasture, the flock of sheep began to drift towards us, like a large, barely sentient cloud. Fido regarded them with attention. He was a miniature spaniel, a breed more noted for hunting birds than herding sheep, but ever since the day at the Screaming Stones he had developed a keen interest in this woolly minded species. Quite obviously he thought they would be great fun to chase.

"No! No! Don't you dare!"

The sheep drifted closer. Several of them baaed. Fido quivered all over.

"No!"

The wind shifted in our direction. Fido evidently got the scent of the flock full in his nostrils, for without another glance in my direction he burst from cover and flung himself upon the sheep, barking joyfully. The sheep reacted with exaggerated alarm, as though a pack of wolves, muzzles wet with lamb's blood, had erupted from the wood; first they bunched up and ran as a group, then they scattered all over the field. Fido was everywhere, running and barking, hysterical with excitement.

Fido had none of the training of a sheep dog, but he could run very, very fast. He ran rings around those sheep, bunching them down into an ever smaller milling, baaing knot of animals.

And in the center of the knot stood Mr. Fredericks and Miss Vincy. There could not have been a more effective method of getting their attention had I been laboring for the past twenty minutes with no other end in view.

Mr. Fredericks made himself heard over the clamor of barking and baaing and the thud of sheep hooves: "Miss Crawley, you might as well cease skulking behind that tree. We know that Fido's presence implies yours. Come out and show yourself."

I ought to have made an appearance, apologized, called my dog and gone away. However, at that moment Miss Vincy cried out in a tone of great distress, "Oh please, Miss Crawley—Althea—come with us if you will, but do not delay us, I beg of you! Every moment is a torment."

"Miss Vincy, what is it?" I asked, emerging from the wood and wading through a river of agitated sheep in order to reach her. "You are ill. You must sit down and rest a moment."

"No! I must go on." She turned and, pushing sheep out of her path, continued to make her way across the field.

I was perplexed, to put it mildly. If this *was* an elopement, it was a queer one, with a third party invited along for the journey.

"Oh, you'll never be happy until you find out what is

stirring, Miss Crawley, so you might as well come too," said Mr. Fredericks. "You may even be able to be of some service to your friend."

With this I had to be content. I hastened my steps to catch Miss Vincy up and, putting my arm around her waist, helped her over the rough ground. So pale was she, and so wild and fearful were her eyes, that it would have been a cruelty to question her further. I held my peace, resolving to get it out of Mr. Fredericks at the first opportunity.

In a few moments we reached our destination: a small workman's cottage with a few outbuildings nearby. What we could want in such a humble dwelling was a mystery to me, but I was not long left in suspense. Miss Vincy burst through the door without knocking and plunged into the darkened interior.

"Has he come? What does he say?" she demanded of a respectable-looking elderly woman who advanced to meet us.

"He's here. Hush, my dear, and we'll know all about it in a moment," responded the woman, an utter stranger to me, though I would have thought I knew by sight every human soul in the district for miles around. Her eyes flicked up to mine. She dropped a curtsey and continued in a low tone, "Pardon my boldness in saying so, Miss

Crawley, but I am glad you've come. My poor dear needs a friend right now."

Bewildered, I followed Miss Vincy into an inner chamber. Our local doctor, Haxhamptonshire, was bending over a tumbled and disordered bed. The figure in the bed was small, that of a young child. As Dr. Haxhamptonshire moved the candle, examining the flushed face and limbs of his patient, I saw it was a little boy, younger even than Alexander.

Miss Vincy sank to her knees by the bed. "Well, Doctor?" she asked in an urgent whisper, "What is it?"

"Ah, Mrs. Annuncio, I see," the doctor said, addressing Miss Vincy. "It is an infection of the lungs. Listen," he said, as the child drew breath. Even I, hesitating in the doorway some ten feet from the bed, could hear a rasping, rattling sound.

"Will he live?" she murmured.

"It's too soon to say. I have given orders to your nurse to give him this syrup, and these powders dissolved in a little warm wine every two hours. You say he has been ailing for the past three days?"

Miss Vincy nodded. "We thought it nothing worse than a cold at first, but he fell into a fever, and I have been so frightened . . ."

"Well, I've seen many worse than this recover—we can only watch and wait."

I had had some experience at nursing, and so as the doctor prepared to leave, I prepared to settle in. Whoever this child was, whoever "Mrs. Annuncio" might be, it was clear that my friend needed me. I instructed Mr. Fredericks to return and tell my mama that I was occupied in helping to nurse a neighbor's child. She would, of course, wish to know which neighbor, so I told him to tell her it was Mrs. Bowden's grandson, come to visit from Scarborough. I added that the doctor believed the disease to be of an infectious nature so I thought it best not to come home until the crisis was over. Old Mrs. Bowden lived quite seven miles away over the moorland, and I doubted Mama would feel the need to hurry over, offering assistance.

As to the rest, I left it to Mr. Fredericks to cope, and I had no doubt that he would.

The little boy was restless and feverish. I set to work bathing his hot forehead with vinegar and water, soothing him as well as I could. The nurse, who, I suspected by her manner, had once been Miss Vincy's own nurse, assisted me ably in my efforts, and after a few hours thus spent, she retired to provide us with a tray of bread and cheese, and the patient with the medicines prescribed by the doctor.

Miss Vincy proved to be inexperienced with children. Her powerful attachment to the boy was the principal difficulty; she fretted and fussed with his bed clothing, smoothed his hair and altogether kept him in a state of perturbation and wakefulness, until I ordered her to cease and desist.

Instead I required her to empty out the satchel she had brought with her, the one I had believed had been packed in anticipation of her flight with Mr. Fredericks. It contained a clean blanket, a stuffed doll for the boy, some common medications, including some paregoric, and a copy of *Delphine*, by Madame de Staël.

"He likes to hear me read aloud," she explained, "no matter what the subject is, so I am accustomed to reading him whatever I happen to be perusing at the moment." I eyed the book with considerable interest, having never been able to get my hands on a copy of a work by the scandalous Frenchwoman before. I rather doubted that a feverish little boy of two years would be able to appreciate her shocking and reprehensible (or so our vicar assures me) meditations on the position of Woman in Society. However, *I* would be interested to hear them, dreadful though they might be, and they could not corrupt the child, since the novel appeared to be written in Madame's native language. It also would keep Miss Vincy occupied, so—

"Pray read it to us," I said. "It will send him to sleep."

In elegant and perfectly accented French, Miss Vincy began to read aloud. My imperfect understanding of that language, as well as the events reported upon by Madame de Staël, ensured my rapt attention. As for Miss Vincy, this tale of a gifted woman who had the courage to defy social conventions seemed to hold special meaning for her. And as I had foretold, the melodious syllables had the effect of putting our patient into a profound sleep, which boded well for his future.

And so the long day passed into night.

Miss Vincy's voice grew ragged, then faltered. I sent her nurse for some tea and took the opportunity of slipping a drop of the paregoric, which has a soporific effect, into her cup. Soon she slept beside the little boy, his hot hand clasped in hers. I could not help but note that the child's hair color was similar to hers, and identical to the small tress in her locket—it was *his* hair she kissed and carried, not the Baron's.

She had not yet told me the child's identity, or his relationship to her, but I had no need to ask, or to pester Mr. Fredericks for information. I knew.

17

MR. FREDERICKS RETURNED EARLY the next morning to enquire after the health of the child, and we were able to give a fairly good account of his night. Leon, for that was his name, lay exhausted and white on the bed, but his huge black eyes were open and aware and the coughing that had racked his small frame was stilled. His cheek was cool (tho' I knew from experience that his fever might rise again, later in the day). He addressed Miss Vincy as "Mama," settling the nature of their relationship beyond a doubt.

His name was a matter of interest to Mr. Fredericks as well. As he accompanied me on a stroll around the farmyard so that I might stretch my cramped limbs, he explained that my stepsister Prudence wished to know what Mrs. Bowden's grandson was called, so that in the event of the boy's death she could create a mourning picture with an affecting verse in his honor.

"She thinks of depicting a tomb and a weeping willow," he said, his face expressionless, "with perhaps a bird flying above to symbolize young Leon's soul escaping into eternity. She hopes you will be able to secure a lock of his hair to incorporate into the composition."

I rolled my eyes. "Thank *goodness* they believe us to be seven miles distant, or she would be here this moment with her sketch paper and crayons, ready to begin memorializing the boy into the grave. I really believe Miss Vincy—" I hesitated and then continued, "I call her that, you know, because she has not told me to call her by any other name—would do her grave bodily injury if she even mentioned the possibility that he might die."

Mr. Fredericks smiled. "I imagine you are right. From all I know of her, I am certain that she is a devoted mother."

I was silent for a moment, thinking. Mr. Fredericks had known enough to bring Miss Vincy to the farmhouse, known that she had a special interest in the child housed therein. Yet he had had to ask the child's name, and had to speculate on her behavior as a parent. Frustrated almost to the fever pitch by convention and good manners, which forbade me to put a few direct questions to him, or to her, I walked a little faster. As I paced I plucked a stalk of flowering weed that brushed against my skirt and began stripping it of its little flowerets, one by one.

I could see nothing of Mr. Fredericks in the little boy's face or form, I realized, and was aware of an intense relief at that knowledge. I could not have *borne* it if he had been that child's father. However, he had known her for a number of years, no doubt stretching back well before the birth of this child. Had he guessed? Or had he known before? He'd spoken admiringly of her likely devotion to a child. Did that mean he admired her in a warmer sense? What *was* the nature of their relationship? I turned to look at him.

He had been watching me, with an amused glint in his eye. He paused and picked another flower head and presented it to me with a bow.

"I see you have done with disassembling that unfortunate blossom, Miss Crawley. Allow me to supply you with another."

I looked down at my hands. Indeed the tiny flowers were all gone and the stalk torn into green strips and discarded. My hands were sticky with sap.

"Oh, ugh! No, I thank you. My hands—"

He gave a positive shout of laughter. "If you could see your face, Miss Crawley! How it maddens you *not to know!* And yet you cannot ask. Here," he added, "use my handkerchief." He handed me a slip of linen, which I inspected suspiciously. True enough, it was covered in ink and other, less identifiable stains. I wiped my fingers on it nonetheless. When I had done he reached for it, but I folded it and put it into my reticule.

"I shall have it laundered and then return it," I said. "I've no doubt it will be a novel experience for the handkerchief."

"Oh, a paltry blow, I fear. Come, come, Miss Crawley, you can do better than that! You wish to know all that *I* know about our mutual friend and the child residing in this place. Very well, I shall tell you all I can." He stopped.

"Yes?"

"I know nothing. I cannot tell you even one thing more than you already know."

"*Oh!*" I turned my back on him and began to walk away. My feelings towards him may have changed, but one thing that had not changed was his ability to stir my ire.

"Temper, Miss Crawley, temper! This display of pique ill suits your station in life, and I have that on the best of authorities. Why, last night," he said, lengthening his stride to catch up to me, "when I informed Mrs. Vincy that her daughter found it necessary to remain at the bedside of some cottager's child, she so forgot herself as to make several inelegant remarks. My dear aunt and mother had all they could do to restrain her. *They* informed her that a lady never loses her temper. And they would know," he added, looking thoughtful. "I believe my uncle, the former baron, *and* my uncle Westing often gave them cause for annoyance."

I slowed my steps. "Really?" I said, diverted by this unexpected insight into the emotional life of a baronial family. I had no difficulty in believing that the late baron had been a trial to his relatives, tho' I'd never met Mr. Westing. But I had always wondered—what *had* life been like for the Fredericks family, living, as I had been given to understand they did, in a room above a shop? "Then . . . did your father never vex Mrs. Fredericks?"

"Frequently. But it was a love match, you know, and went on being one until the day he died. That was the first time I saw my mother really annoyed with him. 'I gave up *everything* for his sake,' said she, 'and *now* he goes off and leaves me!'"

I blushed at my temerity in asking, while repressing a guilty urge to laugh at the image of Mrs. Fredericks scolding her husband for his thoughtlessness in dying. "I am sorry. I ought not to have asked such a . . . such an intrusive question. It must have been a dreadful time for your mother, and for you, being left alone and . . . and perhaps not very well off, at your father's death."

This appeared to fix Mr. Fredericks's attention. He

stopped, and looked at me rather queerly, perhaps over-come by memories.

"Well," he said cautiously, "we were not precisely begging in the streets."

Now I *did* blush. "Of course not!" I said, mortified. "I did not mean you were bound for the poor farm, or anything of that sort!"

"No . . . of course, I don't think they've *got* poor farms in London," he mused, still with that look in his eye. "Soil's not good enough for it, you know, and there are buildings and roads everywhere. Difficult to turn a profit, with crowds of people and horses and carriages trampling your crops all the time."

My eyes narrowed. Perhaps I ought not to have broached the subject, but I could not help but feel he was making use of my honest sympathy for some sort of private jest.

"Then it was lucky, was it not?" I enquired coldly, "that your cousin and aunt were so hospitable as to receive you here in Yorkshire."

He gave another great shout of laughter. "Oh indeed! Now *there* was a famous stroke of good luck for my mama and me!"

"I agree," I said, more coldly still. "I think it was *very* good of the Baron."

The joke, whatever it was, lost its savor. His countenance darkened.

"Yes," he said, "you *would* think that."

We continued on in silence for a few moments. Our conversation seemed to have traveled a long way from the subject of Miss Vincy and her child. Evidently he came to the same conclusion, for at length he said, "I confess I did *not* tell you all I knew about Miss Vincy, as I promised. You perhaps wonder why I brought her here yesterday morning if I was indeed as ignorant as I claim?"

I nodded, but did not speak.

"I've been on intimate terms with the Vincy family for perhaps as much as five years," he said. "Some two and a half or more years ago I became aware of a crisis going on, about which they did not want me to know. Miss Vincy went away, to visit relatives, I was told, and did not return for over a year. Given the old lady's temperament, I found it unsurprising that the daughter should get away when she could, so I said nothing.

"Eventually she turned up again, looking a good bit different. She'd changed, and not for the better. She'd lost something—her nerve, I'd say. She got quieter, and it was a long while before she took up her drawing or painting tools again.

"However, it wasn't until recently, on this visit to York-shire, that I had the opportunity to observe her closely, living in the same household as we are. What I guessed was that she had a secret, a secret that she stole off to visit from time to time. And that it lived in this cottage." He jerked his chin at the house behind us.

"I was curious, I'll admit." He kicked at a stone in his path, frowning. "I've always thought highly of Miss Vincy."

I stared at the stone, feeling my spirits sink.

"When she seemed so agitated lately, I decided to investigate. I stopped by here yesterday morning, early. I asked that woman if I could take any messages to Miss Vincy at Gudgeon Park. She jumped at it. Seems the boy had taken a turn for the worse in the night and she was anxious Miss Vincy know about it. I had a look at the child, so I could convey his condition to her, you know. And then I did the arithmetic. Crisis in the Vincy household two and three-quarters years ago; two-year-old boy kept in a cottage close enough for Miss Vincy to visit regularly.

"I am very good at sums, Miss Crawley," he said. "And this was not a difficult equation."

❧ ❧ ❧

I returned to the house from my walk somewhat refreshed in body but much perturbed in mind. Was this why Mr. Fredericks had not proposed when Mr. Godalming was making a nuisance of himself? A man may be excused for proceeding warily under these circumstances, especially when he does not know all the relevant facts.

Of course, a man may have half a dozen by-blows begat upon half a dozen women without anyone even commenting on the fact, let alone giving his prospective bride cause to reconsider the relationship. But a woman most emphatically may *not*.

My poor Miss Vincy! Did she love Mr. Fredericks, and had she spent yesterday not only in terror for her son but in mourning for the loss of her suitor? Or had she in fact been partial to Lord Boring, as I'd once believed? It occurred to me that, given the speed of recent events, she might not even know of his engagement to Charity. I looked at her as she bent over her son's bed, and I sighed.

She turned white and beckoned me out of the room.

"What? What is it, Miss Crawley? Do you see something I do not? He seems so much better today."

"No, no, no," I assured her. "I quite agree. He is going on very well."

"Then why did you look so sad, and sigh?"

I should have been quite happy to have passed it off

with an excuse, but she was remorseless. She was determined to know the truth, and, with a worried mother's single-mindedness, she assumed it had to do with her sick child. At last I said, "It was for quite a different cause, I assure you. I was thinking of Lord Boring and Charity."

She stared at me blankly. At least I could be certain that Lord Boring had been little in her thoughts of late. "Lord Boring . . . and Miss Charity Winthrop? But why should they make you sad?"

"Oh, not sad, exactly. In fact," I said, "it is quite happy news. They are to be married."

Her eyes, so like Leon's, grew enormous. "Miss Crawley! Althea, dear. I am so, so sorry! How selfish of me. Here you have been, wearing yourself out on our account, when you must be wretched. I feared it would happen, but I hoped you would not mind too much."

I smiled and assured her that I did not mind at all. She frowned and looked doubtful, whereupon I said, "I *did* mind, at first. But I do not believe he is to be regretted. He is not the man I thought he was. But I was afraid that *you* might be upset by it."

"*I*? But why should I be upset?" And she looked so startled by the idea that I saw that there had never been a partiality on her side, only on her mother's. "Althea—that is, Miss Crawley . . ."

"No, I beg you will please call me by my first name."

"And you must call me Hephzibah. Surely you must realize that Lord Boring never had the slightest intention of marrying me, however rich my papa is?"

"But, but . . . ah . . . Hephzibah, I feared that you might wish it, nevertheless."

Miss Vincy burst out into a peal of laughter. "How funny it sounds! No one ever calls me Hephzibah, no one! Even Mr. Annuncio did not."

"Mr. Annuncio—? Oh! You mean . . ."

Miss Vincy, or rather Hephzibah, ceased laughing. "Yes," she said. "Mr. Annuncio. My husband."

18

"MR. ANNUNCIO WAS THE drawing master," explained the lady I now knew to be Mrs. Annuncio, also known as Miss Vincy and Hephzibah.

"Ah," I said.

"We were legally married, tho' it was 'over the anvil' in Scotland, not by a minister in a church, and my son is legitimate, tho' unrecognized as such by his grandparents. His grandfather would like to see him, I know, but my mother will not allow it."

"They know of Leon's existence, then."

"Oh, yes. Keeping Leon a secret from everyone else was made a condition of my being taken back into their household. My mother covered my flight so well that not a word about the marriage escaped. She convinced her aunt, who is dependent upon her, and who lives quite out of society, to say that I was on an extended visit to her home. Of course, my parents do *not* know that I had Leon conveyed here to Yorkshire and installed nearby where I could visit him from time to time. I could not bear to be parted from him, and so I gave my old nurse, who was caring for him, some jewelry to sell to finance his journey and housing, and arranged to have him follow me north. That is," she went on, "I suppose that since Mr. Fredericks told them I was tending a child nearby, they do know, or at least they must guess that it is so."

"I see. And your husband is now . . . ?"

"In his grave," she replied calmly. "When you enquired some weeks ago about the present whereabouts of my former tutor I told the truth in saying that I did not know. I am not certain of the exact location of his remains, only that he is no more. It did not last long as a marriage. He was a bad husband and a worse father. On the other hand," she said, with a reminiscent gleam in her eye, "as a draughtsman he was superb. He could draw anything, either from life or from memory. And as a colorist—"

As touching as this tribute to her late husband's professional skills was, I interrupted.

"You were not with him when he died, then?"

"No. He was disappointed when my mother refused to have anything to do with me after the marriage. He had hoped that my being with child would reconcile her to the match, but when he realized it would not, he abandoned me, and his unborn son."

"Oh, my dear Miss Vi—that is, er, Hephzibah . . ."

She laughed. "Never mind, Althea. You may go back to calling me Miss Vincy if you prefer. We are both used to it, and I do not go by my married name, for obvious reasons."

"Oh, *thank* you," I said. "I cannot think of you as a Hephzibah, somehow. But what did you do, Miss Vincy? Did your parents take you back once they knew your husband had left you?" This seemed unlikely, as Mr. Fredericks claimed she had been gone from her family home for over a year.

She cocked her head at a soft sound in the boy's bedroom, and went to stand over his bed. She was clearly intending to take her place at his side once more, but I objected.

"Really, Miss Vincy, we ought to let him get some sleep. Our talking will disturb him, and he will do very well without your constant presence. We shall only be a room away, you know."

"Ah, but I have been so close to losing him in the past few days, and in general I can spend so little time with him that I must make the most of it. Well, he does appear to be resting, so perhaps we should both take some tea and continue our talk in the next room."

We were shortly provided with tea, in rough earthenware mugs, true, but hot and comforting, and some bread with butter and honey. When Nurse Braddock had retired, I ventured to continue my catechism.

"Perhaps you *did* go to stay with your great-aunt when your husband left you, thereby making your mother's story true?" I suggested.

"Oh, no. My mother was far too angry with me, and Great-Aunt Anne would never have done anything to annoy her. When Mr. Annuncio and I returned from Scotland after our wedding, such as it was, he brought me back to London. He had married me, of course, for my money, and my money—that is, my family—was in London.

"As an artist, he had a circle of friends and acquaintances including a number of working portrait painters. When he deserted me, several of them were kind enough to help me by sending me some commissions, so that I might scrape a living painting miniatures on ivory. I managed to support first myself alone and then myself and Leon, by means of this work.

"It was one of his friends, a kind, good man named Drury, who discovered that Mr. Annuncio was dead, and went to the Whitechapel slum where he had been knifed in a fight. Mr. Drury saw him buried, and paid for it too."

She put her mug of tea down and was silent a moment.

"I—I am sorry," I said.

"Oh, *I* am not," she replied. "Tho' it is true that the world lost a fine painter. Had he lived he would have bled me white. He would appear from time to time, you know, demanding money. No, that sailor who killed him did me a great favor, and my son too. And when he was dead I was able to write to my parents. I could never have been reconciled to them while he lived, and I am quite fond of them. Of *both* of them," she added.

I did not reply to this at once, for I was thinking. "Was it . . . was it so very dreadful, being a woman alone, earning your living in London?"

"No . . . in some ways I enjoyed it, tho' it was a fearsome struggle much of the time. And of course I had my son with me every moment, as I do not have him now. But Leon has never been strong. I could not neglect any chance to improve the conditions of his daily life. The neighborhood in which we resided was not ideal for a delicate child."

I sat musing for a moment. If I had a talent like Miss Vincy's, and no young brother or mother for whom I must save an estate, would I have the courage to live alone and independent? Then, if I ever *did* choose to marry, I could marry someone I liked and respected, without reference to his fortune. Someone who could make me laugh, for instance. Someone like . . .

However, I did *not* have a talent like Miss Vincy's and I *did* have a mother and young brother who dearly needed me to marry well, so it was not worth thinking of. Perhaps one day women might be able to choose their husbands with no thought of money and position, but not in this day and age in Lesser Hoo, Yorkshire, England.

"My life is quite tolerable, by and large," Miss Vincy was saying, "except that I see my son less than I would wish. I did have to promise my mother that I would marry any man of whom she approved, if she could maneuver him into asking, but I felt that I would be able to discourage most men from asking. Unfortunately, somehow or other Mr. Godalming got the idea that I was open to his advances. I do not know how it was that you got rid of him, Althea, but I am most grateful."

The mortification which smote me may be imagined. "Oh, really, I had nothing to do with it," I muttered, feebly repulsing her attempt to show her thankfulness by kissing me. "It was entirely Mr. Fredericks's doing."

I next had to listen to an effusion about what a

staunch friend and all-in-all splendid fellow Mr. Fredericks was. In the faint hope of disillusioning her, I explained *how* he had discouraged Mr. Godalming, but she laughed merrily and shook her head at his cunning.

"I shall have to remember that!" she said. "Tho' perhaps poor Papa would prefer I not use it too often."

❧ ❧ ❧

Dr. Haxhamptonshire called that afternoon and pronounced Leon to be well on the road to recovery. His temperature remained low for the rest of the afternoon, and it was determined that Miss Vincy and I would return on the morrow to our respective abodes.

The good doctor was warned not to call Miss Vincy by her married name again ("I only told him, because I did not wish him to look down on my son as illegitimate, and perhaps not exert himself to do everything he could," she explained), and I thought he would obey, if only because a man as rich as Mr. Vincy and a woman as determined as Mrs. Vincy could cause him serious harm, even here in our quiet little corner of the world.

We ate a humble but hearty meal, and spent the evening with the invalid, who was awake and beginning to be interested in some warm gruel. Nurse Braddock sat with us and revealed herself to be a good, decent soul, fond of Miss Vincy and of young Leon. We whiled away the evening listening to her tales of Miss Vincy's infancy and early years—I had little difficulty believing that she was a perfect paragon of goodness, and clever with her crayons—and went early to bed.

As neither of us had had the forethought to bring a change of clothes along on our visit, and as we did not wish our families to know where we were, Mr. Fredericks had been authorized to bring us the necessities so that we might present a dignified and decent appearance. To give greater color to the story that we had been staying at some distance, he then undertook to drive me by coach to the castle before returning Miss Vincy to the Park, even tho' it was but a twenty-minute walk for me and fifteen for Miss Vincy.

We washed and dressed ourselves with as much care as possible and awaited his arrival. Master Leon was up this morning and toddling about, pestering his mother and his nurse to be allowed to go out of doors. Beyond the fact that he was new-risen from a sickbed, the day was rainy and blustery; he was instructed not to think of such a thing, but to play with his toys quietly in front of the fire.

But the morning wore away and Mr. Fredericks did

not come. By noon Leon had exhausted his newfound vigor and become tired and peevish. He wept and coughed and clung to his mother, whom he rightly suspected was preparing to leave him. Nurse Braddock fed him some porridge with cream and his mama rocked him to sleep.

Miss Vincy laid her son down upon his bed and we waited, in a mood which alternated (at least for me) between annoyance and foreboding. Outside, the wind and rain lashed against the walls of the cottage, and through the windows we could see branches heaving back and forth.

"Perhaps Mr. Fredericks thinks the weather too bad to venture out," suggested Miss Vincy.

I did not trouble to reply to this. Mr. Fredericks was not afraid of a little bad weather, and Miss Vincy knew it quite well. She was trying to persuade herself out of any unkind thoughts about him. Now would be the best possible time for her to leave, while her little boy slept. I knew she was torn, wishing to stay with him, to satisfy herself that all was as well with him as she believed, but she was also anxious to return to her parents and soothe their ruffled feelings and calm their fears. She bit her lip and watched the window and the small yard in front of the cottage.

I was occupied in preparing a scolding for Mr. Fred-

ericks when he should finally arrive, until it suddenly occurred to me that there might be a reason beyond simple
perversity for this delay. Perhaps he was ill. I remembered
that he *had* been ill on his return from India. I wondered,
as I never had before, about the nature of that illness, and
how serious it had been. What if he was at this moment
tossing with fever?

Or perhaps there had been an accident? He was a
superb horseman, but accidents may happen even to the
skilled. Pictures flashed across my mind, of Mr. Fredericks lying in a gully with a broken neck, of Lord Boring's
horses and carriage careening off a cliff.

"Althea, is something wrong? You have torn that
handkerchief quite in half," said Miss Vincy. "And your
face is whiter than the handkerchief."

I looked down. It was true. I had spoilt a perfectly
good handkerchief. I began to reassure Miss Vincy, but
was interrupted by the sound of hoofs and the jingle
of harness in the road outside. We started up from our
chairs and hurried to the door in time to hear Mr. Fredericks's voice halting the horses and to see him, wearing a
greatcoat of such smartness and with such a multiplicity
of capes that it was almost certainly the property of Lord
Boring, jumping down from the box.

Relief washed over me with such intensity that I realized I had been digging my fingernails into my palms for the past two hours. "Where have you been?" I demanded.

"Do not fly at me, I pray you, Miss Crawley," he said, shaking the rainwater off himself all over the room, its contents and its occupants, like a large, wet dog. "I give you both my apologies for being so late. I had my reasons." Although he was ostensibly speaking to me, his gaze was fixed on Miss Vincy, and he did not so much as glance in my direction during the following exchanges.

Since it seemed clear that he was not going to tell me those reasons, or at least not at present, I enquired after our clothing and other effects he had promised to bring.

"Oh, I forgot them," he said. "Well, nothing is to be done about it now, I suppose. Are you ready? Miss Vincy?"

I was opening my mouth to berate him for this cavalier attitude, but something about the steadfast way in which he refused to look at me was unsettling.

"Is something wrong?" I asked, in a gentler tone.

"No, not at all," he informed the top of Miss Vincy's head. "Or rather, that is to say, yes, very much so. I've had a devil of a quarrel with Boring, and I intend to clear out as soon as I've delivered the two of you."

"Clear out!" we cried in unison. Miss Vincy, remembering her sleeping son, hushed us, and the ensuing conversation took place in whispers.

"But you and Lord Boring are such great friends!" murmured Miss Vincy.

"No longer," retorted Mr. Fredericks. "If I didn't think duels were nothing but a waste of good ammunition, I swear I'd . . . Never mind. I'm off, and that lot at the Park can manage without my assistance."

"But . . . but where will you go?" I asked, feeling as tho' an arrow had pierced my heart.

At this, his eyes shifted to mine for one brief moment, and I feared I may have allowed my emotion to appear in my voice.

"Doesn't much matter, does it?" Then he bent his gaze once again on Miss Vincy.

"Well? Are you ready or not?" he said, and his tone was so savage that we gathered our shawls and bonnets and climbed into the coach in a meek silence.

19

SO BRIEF WAS OUR drive that we scarce had time to settle ourselves, trade puzzled looks, and consider how to debate the matter, before we jerked to a halt, the carriage door was wrenched open and Mr. Fredericks was handing me out into the side yard of the castle.

He was still not looking at me.

I caught his sleeve in a firm grip.

"Mr. Fredericks, I pray you," I said earnestly. "Can you not see that you are frightening me? What is amiss between you and Lord Boring? And how does it affect me, or the ones I love? For I can see that it does," I added, when he made as if to wave this away.

"I assure you—" he began, but I interrupted him.

"Whatever it is that you are about to assure me of *will not do*. Come, Mr. Fredericks, we have become friends, I hope, over these past weeks. Please pay me the compliment of treating me as a rational being, as you always have done."

The sky, overcast and storm-tossed since dawn, darkened abruptly to a greenish gray. The horses tossed their heads and nickered uneasily. With a suddenness that made it seem as though someone above us on one of the castle parapets had upended a barrel of water over our heads, it began to rain very hard indeed. Mr. Fredericks uttered an outraged sputter as rivulets of water coursed down his neck.

"What the deuce do you mean by keeping us standing here in this downpour, madam?" he demanded. As if cued by his exclamation, a flash of lightning flickered on the horizon, followed almost immediately afterwards by a deafening roll of thunder. The moat, already high, was now at flood stage.

"I mean to get the answer to my question, sir," I replied, much relieved to hear him relapse into his usual tone of familiar incivility, "and I will, even tho' the waters of the North Sea rise up and drown us where we stand."

Audibly grinding his teeth he said, "Oh, very well. I only learned of his betrothal to that long drink of vinegar, Miss Charity Winthrop, this morning. I told him it was a disgrace, when—"

C-r-r-ack! Bang-bang-crash!

Simultaneous with this stupendous noise, a white-hot finger of fire leapt from a cloud to that easternmost castle's turret, which overhung the cliff. I clapped my hands to my ears, thus losing my grip on Mr. Fredericks's sleeve. He took the opportunity to steer me towards the castle gate.

"Get inside!" he said, raising his voice over the boom of thunder. "You'll be fried like a sausage on a stick if you don't get under cover."

"So will you and Miss Vincy," I retorted. "You can't keep driving in a storm like this. You must put the carriage in the stables and wait it out."

"We'll be—"

Our quarreling was interrupted by a dreadful grating, rending sound. We turned in unison, and saw.

The waters of the moat had, as Mr. Fredericks had predicted, burst through their restraining walls and now poured in two fountains down the cliff face towards the sea. The land that jutted out over the sea and held up the east wing of the castle began to move. From a solid mass it liquefied, resolving itself into thousands of rocks and clods of earth which abruptly . . . disappeared. We heard a noise like a roaring waterfall as it fell, then a great crash as it hit the beach below. After an interval, a cloud of airborne dirt mushroomed up, to hover over the castle and rain mud down upon us.

A good third of the castle's eastern wing hung over the abyss, unsupported.

Someone was screaming. I turned to my companion with a word of reproach on my lips.

"Good Gad!" he said, his face white (tho' liberally bespattered with filth) in the lurid light. "Stop that squawking, Miss Crawley," he added. "Haven't our eardrums been insulted enough already?"

I, squawking? *I, I*—I opened and closed my mouth several times in rapid succession, but nothing came out.

C-r-r-r-ack!

"There she goes," said Mr. Fredericks softly.

I shifted my gaze from his visage back to the castle. *"No!"*

A dark line had appeared on the castle walls where it hung out over the cliff, running from top to bottom. The mortar bonding the stones disintegrated and fell in a fine shower of powder. The entire eastern wing of the castle shimmered, sagged, and then crumbled, tipping the easternmost portion with the lightning-struck turret over into the sea.

To my everlasting shame, the first words out of my mouth, when once the reverberations of this second crash had faded, were: *"We just paid to have that roof repaired!"*

Miss Vincy leaned from the carriage to cry, "Oh Althea! Your mother and sisters and your little brother! The servants! And how dreadful if someone were on the beach below!"

I gasped in mortification. What a monster of parsimony and avarice I was! How *could* I have thought of pounds and pence before human lives?

"Well, as to that," said Mr. Fredericks, "I'll warrant no one save the three of us would be foolish enough to be out of doors in this weather, so I doubt anyone was on the beach to be injured. However, we'd better determine the whereabouts of the rest of your list and see what the damage is."

We were spared this exertion, however, by the eruption over the drawbridge of every inhabitant of Crooked Castle, from Mama and Prudence (Charity, we discovered, was visiting her fiancé's family at the Park) to Greengages and the little scullery maid. Only young Tom, the kitchen boy, was injured, having been struck by a falling stone. He was carried out, much enjoying the attention, and the general belief seemed to be that he was suffering from a severe bruise rather than a broken bone.

The lack of injuries was less surprising than it seemed. The east wing was a cold, damp place in this weather. We rarely used it in the best of times except for Mama's and my bedrooms. Since it was early afternoon, no one had any reason to have been in it, those two rooms having been tidied hours earlier.

The household milled around in the castle yard, reluctant to reenter the building until some sense of the present and future danger could be gained. As we counted off noses, ensuring that all were present and accounted for, our neighbors began to appear, in twos and threes.

The violent storm soon cleared out, leaving a pale blue sky and a smell of damp vegetation. We were therefore able to conduct our business in the open air, portioning off our servants to various houses in the area. Greengages was to go to his daughter, who lived in the village, Cook to her sister, and so on. The vicar, Mr. Bold, was good enough to busy himself in the matter and soon all were assured of a hot meal and a bed.

Miss Vincy was now in the awkward position of wishing to insist that Mama, Alexander, Prudence, and I join Charity at Gudgeon Park, while being herself a guest and unable to do so. Mr. Fredericks had no such scruples.

"Mrs. Winthrop, Miss Crawley, and Master Crawley, as well as Miss Winthrop, will all be housed at Gudgeon Park," he announced.

I gathered breath to point out that he was no longer in a position (if he ever had been) to dictate who would or would not be housed at the Park, and to protest that I would be much happier to be accommodated at Yellering Hall, but remembered that it was shut up and the servants put on board wages while the Throstletwists visited their son and daughter-in-law in Hull.

"Yes, Althea, really you must," murmured Miss Vincy. "With the engagement between Miss Charity and Lord Boring, you are soon to be closely connected with the family at the Park. It would look odd if you did not go to them under the circumstances."

Mama concurred, and, as Lord Boring and the Marquis appeared on horseback and made the invitation official, it was so decided. I insisted on going into the stricken castle in order to retrieve a few items of a personal nature for myself and my relatives, spurning Mr. Fredericks's advice on the subject. I had gone for two days without an opportunity to refresh my costume and did not propose to continue in the same manner for yet another day, no matter how risky the venture. Since it was my and my mother's bedchambers that had tumbled into the sea, I purloined one or two things from Charity and Prudence's room to make up the deficiency.

We all crowded into the carriage and were soon splashing down the road towards the Park. Being under the impression that I would be in company with Lord

Boring for the first time since he proposed to Charity, everyone eyed me with expressions ranging from avid curiosity (Prudence) to sympathy and concern (Mama and Miss Vincy). While it was true that I had rather not be obliged to stay at the Park just now, I did not wish anyone to believe it was an especial grief to me, rather than simply embarrassing. I therefore forced myself to smile, and observed that it certainly was good to have kind neighbors when disaster struck.

Doubtfully, they agreed that it was.

"And we shall be able to see Charity in all her glory," I added. "What a handsome baroness she will make, will she not?"

None of them answered. They simply looked at me. I was only sorry that Mr. Fredericks, being outside on the box driving, could not witness my performance.

❧ ❧ ❧

Mrs. Westing could not in common humanity avoid receiving us with some pretence of concern, and she paused in one of her eternal games of patience long enough to see to it that we were given rooms.

"When you are come down again we shall play a little faro," she proposed, with an acquisitive gleam in her eye.

"I feel we are being marked down as a pair of likely gulls in a gaming club," I whispered to Mama as we mounted the stairs. "Thank goodness it is well known that we have no money to lose."

"Hush," murmured Mama, trying to repress a nervous laugh. "I am afraid your last remark is more true than ever. Oh, Althea, whatever shall we do?"

She was right, of course. Our future did look grim. There would be a huge bill for repairs to the castle, always assuming it could be repaired. And we had lost the Baron, and Charity's fortune, in one stroke.

"Never fear, dearest," I said, giving her a quick hug. "I shall think of something; I always do."

Mama and Alexander were to share a room. I, at Miss Vincy's invitation, was to move into her quarters. I was pleased to do so; I remembered what Mr. Fredericks had said about her leaving soon, now that she was not to marry the Baron, and I knew I would miss her dreadfully.

Prudence and Charity would sleep in the same room. Poor Prudence! Soon she would lose her sister and confidante to marriage. Once Charity became a permanent part of the Park household I doubted she would spare much time for her sister, or for her erstwhile best friend, Miss Hopkins. However, Prudence did not appear to be at all cast down. She had asked for her collection of memento mori and her pens, paints, brushes and some paper to be brought from the castle, so she did not mean to be idle. Since my patient, whom she believed to be Mrs. Bowden's grandchild seemed unlikely to die, thus providing a fit subject for her talents, perhaps she could turn them to a lighter subject and do something to commemorate her sister's engagement.

Surprisingly, when we went downstairs again to join the others, we found Mr. Fredericks glowering in a corner of the sitting room and there seemed to be no immediate expectation of his departure. The subject was not raised, nor did Lord Boring go and speak to him, seeming, if anything, a little nervous in his presence. Mrs. Fredericks on the other hand was her usual imperturbable self, bustling about and offering refreshments. It occurred to me for the first time to wonder whether she would stay on if her son left.

I supposed she would. Mr. Fredericks had said that they were not destitute at his father's death, but their establishment in London cannot have compared with Gudgeon Park, and once he left his cousin's employ he was unlikely to be able to support her. In any case, her sister and nephew depended on her to organize their lives and run their household. Charity, I felt sure, would be only too happy to relinquish any and all duties to such an amiable and accomplished housekeeper, whose services could be retained for the cost of her meals and a few hand-me-down clothes.

Mrs. Fredericks made what seemed to be a special effort to welcome me, no doubt out of sympathy for my destitute state, bereft both of home and suitor, and I appreciated it.

"Ah, my little mermaid," she said. "Wet again! Come here into the conservatory and I will comb and dry your hair."

I sat upon a stool at her knee and she tended to my hair as gently as my mother would have done. Meanwhile, I thought about her son. What would happen to him? Not for the first time I regretted the lack of an inquisitive and sophisticated male relation who could have enquired about the specifics of Mr. Fredericks's financial standing in the world. If only he had even a small independence! In that case. . . Why, in that case, I believe I would have done everything in my power to make him love me. It was therefore best I did not know—no small independence would rescue my family now.

He had quarreled with Lord Boring because His Lordship had become betrothed to Charity. Most likely that meant that he had wanted and expected his cousin to marry Miss Vincy. I sighed. Certainly he was fond of her, and she of him.

Would *he* marry Miss Vincy, perhaps fulfilling the same post for her father that he had for Lord Boring? If so, I would not see him again, or not for a great many years, at least, as the Vincys lived in London.

Looking through the conservatory door, I could see him in the dark corner where he sat, moodily stabbing at a small hole in the Axminster carpet with the end of a walking stick.

Normally when we visited at the Park he was busy working, only to be seen striding towards his office in the rear portion of the house with untidy masses of paper protruding from his pockets, or else holed up in that chilly, cheerless cubbyhole, scribbling away, sending messenger boys with missives to the London post. Now he sat and did nothing, while we all studied him out of the corners of our eyes.

For I was not the only one stealing a look at him from time to time. When Mrs. Fredericks had finished braiding and putting up my hair we rejoined the party in the drawing room. I soon realized that with the exception of his mother and my mother the rest of the assembled company was watching him. Lord Boring did, with a worried frown. Mrs. Westing watched him also, and even Charity—yes, I was sure of it—even *Charity* cast nervous glances in his direction.

Yet he sat on, sublimely unaware of all this covert attention, poking away at the hole in the rug. At last, unable to bear it, I got up and took his stick away from him.

"This carpet at least is not a copy, unlike our tapestries," I said to him in an undertone. "Pray do not destroy it."

He looked startled, and his eye fell upon the mischief he had wrought. "You're right," he said. "I'm good for nothing today." And he got up and asked his mother in a low voice to have some bread and cheese sent up to his room in lieu of dinner.

Once he had retired I gradually realized that the focus of attention in the room had shifted. I could not be mistaken. All through dinner, all through a lengthy game of faro, which we played for pennies, as Mrs. Westing declared herself unable to enjoy a game in which no money at *all* was hazarded, all through the long hours until we could excuse ourselves, clutching the few farthings that remained to us, and retire to our borrowed chambers, yes, all that long time, the entire household, both guests and hosts, was now watching *me*.

20

THE NEXT MORNING I escaped any further scrutiny by coming downstairs very early, leaving a note behind me on my pillow to explain that I had gone back to the castle to view how it had weathered the night. Then I crept out of doors without being seen by any of the servants. Fido and I walked swiftly down the drive.

As is often the case after a powerful, destructive storm, it was an achingly beautiful day. Even so late in the summer, I could still hear the occasional skylark singing, and the fields were speckled with red poppies. I saw as we walked along that ours was not the only family to have suffered damage, spying downed trees and once-tidy farmyards turned to boggy marshes. The farmers were hard at work already, sawing up limbs and adding to their woodpiles for the winter.

None of this beauty or industry lifted my spirits, however. I felt as tho' I moved along in my own little dark cloud of despond, and when I arrived at the castle, the gloom only deepened.

The cliff face had crumbled still further, dragging more of my home with it into oblivion. Now the castle, which had been built in the shape of a knobby, lop-sided square, was shaped like a capital E with the middle stroke missing. The entire east wing was gone, as was the land that had once supported it.

"Take care, Miss Crawley, the ground's none too stable near the edge." It was Jock, also come to assess the damage. "You can see there've been more rock falls in the night."

"Oh, Jock!" I cried, and could speak no more.

He understood me well enough, though. If it had been permissible between the young mistress and a servant, he would have patted my arm. As it was, he nodded and tugged at his forelock. "Yes, miss," he said.

I sighed. "We shall have to think what is to be done," I said. "But at present, I believe I would like a moment or two alone."

"Yes, miss." And he went away.

I sat down on an outcropping of stone a safe distance from the scene of the disaster, careless of the effect this might have on my dress. Fido, sensing my desolation, crawled into my lap and, slowly and methodically, licked my hand all over. I sat like this for a long time, not thinking much, but becoming aware that I had eaten nothing since dinner the night before, and wondering if my favorite shawl had gone over the cliff in the night with the rest of my wardrobe.

"I told you it was a foolish place to build," said a voice in my ear. "I cannot imagine what possessed your great-grandfather to do such a thing. And the folly of digging that moat! It weakened already unstable ground to the point of disaster."

I did not turn to look at Mr. Fredericks, for my tears were flowing freely. I said nothing.

"The rest will follow it into the sea in the next year or two," he persisted. "Give it up, Miss Crawley."

Something shifted under the castle, causing an internal floor to cant seaward. Three of our decrepit chairs slowly slid down the slope and fell to the beach below.

"Do you see?"

At this I *did* turn, still saying nothing.

He recoiled at the sight of my (no doubt) reddened, wet, and swollen face.

"You're not crying, are you?"

"Of course I am crying, Mr. Fredericks!" I replied, exasperated. "What else would you have me do?"

"But you mustn't do *that!* I had no idea you would *cry* about it."

"I am made of flesh and blood like other women, Mr. Fredericks. How did you think I would react?"

He seemed a bit at a loss. "Well . . . I thought you would be annoyed with *me*, as you usually are."

"Other than your monumental lack of tact in coming here to rub salt into my wounds, I do not see what you have to do with it, sir," I said. "How would my being angry with you have helped in any way?"

Again he thought this over. "It would have cheered *me* up, at any rate," he said at last.

"In that case, I apologize for not considering your entertainment," I said. "I was distracted for the moment, thinking about Alexander's future, as well as my mother's." *And my own.*

He was silent a moment. "You do realize, don't you," he said, "that Bumbershook has been getting his nerve up to propose to your mother for the past fortnight? This'll tip him over the edge," he added, gesturing at the ravaged castle. "Hah! 'Tip him over the edge'! That's quite good."

"What?"

"Of course. The only thing that's stopped him so far is the tremendous stink it'll cause amongst the members of the *ton*. They're a terrific bunch of snobs, that lot. You're nobody, you see, you and your mother," he explained helpfully, "and there's hardly any money."

"But . . . the Marquis of Bumbershook and . . . my mother?"

"You're not very observant, are you?" he said. "They've been inseparable all summer long."

"True . . ." I admitted. "But then, Alexander—"

"I've advised him to adopt the boy. He has no other children."

"Oh! You have?"

"Yes, and then of course . . . well, you see there's something else, something that might have an effect on all this." He broke off and turned away from me. Looking more awkward and self-conscious than I had ever seen him, he picked up a stick from the ground, which he threw for Fido.

Fido leapt enthusiastically from my lap and raced off after it. Mr. Fredericks stood with his back to me, watching the dog as he ran.

"What is it?" I asked, as he seemed to have dropped the subject.

"What is what?"

"The 'something else' that might have an effect on the Marquis marrying my mother and adopting my brother," I reminded him.

"Oh yes. Well . . . *my* marriage. I'd never intended to marry, you know, but lately, I have been thinking I might, if the lady were willing, at any rate."

I fell silent. Was he confiding in me about Miss Vincy? How could his marriage to her affect my mother's to the Marquis?

The wind was picking up, and tendrils of hair blew across my face. I used this as an excuse to shield my eyes from his gaze with my hand. The silence stretched out, longer and longer. Fido barked off in the distance.

"Marriage to whom?" I said, at the exact same moment *he* said, "Damn that dog! He's far too close to the edge."

I rose from my seated position in alarm and looked where he was pointing. True enough, Fido was perilously close to the insecure rim of the precipice.

"Fido!" I cried, "Come back here at once!"

Fido paid no attention to this admonition whatsoever, as he was barking madly at a squirrel in a tree.

"Fool dog!" Both Mr. Fredericks and I said in unison. We broke into a run, calling his name in angry tones. At length, unable to see the squirrel any longer, he ran back to us, wagging his tail amiably.

Mr. Fredericks found a length of string in his pockets which he used to secure Fido, and we walked back to the rock where we had been sitting. Some of the tension of our conversation had dispersed.

"Idiot beast," he observed. "I ought never to have given him to you. He's a perfect nuisance sometimes."

"Mr. Fredericks," I said, gathering up my courage, "you were speaking of your . . . your possible marriage."

"I was," he admitted. "Look, you've led a sheltered life here in this small village out in the middle of nowhere, Miss Crawley. You may not realize the difference that money makes."

My jaw dropped open. "I? *I* may not realize the difference that money makes? *I?*"

He looked at me uneasily. "Perhaps you do, then," he muttered. "It's only that, marriage, you know, requires—"

My patience snapped. "Are you attempting to say, in your inimitable fashion, sir, that you cannot offer for my hand in marriage because I am too poor? If so, I beg you will desist, because—" Here I broke off and began to sob noisily.

"What? No! Oh, in the name of all that's wonderful, she's crying again! Stop that at once, I tell you!"

"I will not!" I shouted at him, tears splashing down my cheeks. "And what do you mean that *you* ought never to have given me Fido? You didn't! The Baron gave him to me."

"He most certainly did not!" Mr. Fredericks roared, growing red in the face. "I chose that pup, and paid a pretty penny for him, I might add. *I* paid! I always pay! Haven't you worked that out by now?"

I stopped crying and stared at him.

"Yes, you . . . you *great booby*! Everything at Gudgeon Park that is new or beautiful or even useful is there because *I* have paid for it. Every chair, every carpet, every silver candlestick, every kitchen knife! Boring's a bit short of the ready, didn't you know? The pair of them have hardly a pound I haven't given them."

He picked up another stick and began to slice at the grass with it. "Not his fault, really," he said in a more composed tone of voice. "His uncle didn't leave him much scratch to begin with, and then that mother of his is an inveterate gambler. The money that woman has run through! He was most thankful to get her away from London, up to the country where gambling stakes run more towards shillings than pounds.

"I let people believe it was his money behind the Park. Why not? I had no house myself and didn't need one. In fact, I've mostly preferred people *not* know my income and influence. And he was good to me when we were boys, at a time when he need not have been kind. But he has barely enough money to pay the servants, let alone refurnish the place. That's why . . ." he broke off, and raised his eyes to mine for one brief moment, and then dropped them again.

"That is why," he continued, prodding at a stone with his stick in much the way he had bedeviled the carpet the night before, "Boring *had* to marry for money. He had to, and I had no quarrel with that, until he began distinguishing you in that very open manner. I thought . . . we all believed he was madly, hopelessly in love, and proposed to forfeit the estate, give up everything, in order to marry you.

"Well, you appeared to return his affections, so there seemed nothing to be done about it. And your mother was so *dense* about understanding when people tried to hint at his financial situation. I believe he *did* love you, but then . . . well, practicalities intervened. Real life, and real responsibilities, as presented by Mrs. Westing, mostly. She'd hoped to get her hands on Vincy's fortune, of course, but Miss Vincy doesn't want to marry, and Boring hasn't the brains or character to appreciate her, so—"

I interrupted. "You say that Miss Vincy does not wish to marry. Not even . . . not even you? She is very fond of you."

He looked up, surprised. "Me? Lord no. She's fond of me, yes, as I am of her. But marriage? Never. She's had an unfortunate experience—well, you know that! She no more wants to marry me than she does that young idiot Godalming. All she wants to do is to be left alone to paint. Nor have I the least desire to marry her, as much as I like and admire her."

I shook my head slowly, trying to clear it.

"I do not understand. The Baron and Mrs. Westing, poor, and you, whom I believed to be merely your cousin's man of business, rich? Where did the money come from? I beg your pardon for my curiosity, but I really feel I must know."

"Some from my father, of course, but—"

"Wait! Your father was but an employee in a shop, or so I have always been told."

"To begin with, yes. The owner went bankrupt, my father bought him out, shillings on the pound, and so he got his start. My mother was no fool. She knew he was a clever man, and an ambitious one, when she ran away with him. It wasn't for his beauty she admired him, I can tell you."

"But I thought that that was exactly why—"

Mr. Fredericks paused and pulled a locket out of his pocket. He opened it to reveal two miniature portraits. "This," he said, pointing to the lady, "is my mother as a young woman. The other is my father."

"Oh! My! Yes, yes, I see what you mean. Presumably there must have been some other quality that attracted her."

"He was a great businessman, my father. By the time he died he owned a string of shops and was in negotiations to purchase a ship-building company. And I have . . ." Here he paused and looked down modestly. "I have rather built on his successes. I now own most of his original businesses, several carpet and cloth looming manufactories, three banks, a sizeable fleet of ships, several sail makers, two lumberyards, and a button factory."

"A—a button factory?" was all I could think of to say. "I didn't know such a thing existed."

"Yes, clothing and textiles—they're all going to be made in factories in the future. That's the way to make clothing affordable. And a button factory speeds the process."

"Really? How . . . how extraordinary."

"Yes, and I have been neglecting business all summer, hanging about up here on what might as well be the back side of the moon (tho' I *have* made some progress towards establishing a cotton mill in York, and Vincy and I have done a little tea trading as well) because, well, because I wanted to see what would happen to you."

"To me?"

"Yes. I assumed you would marry Boring, of course, but if you didn't, well . . ."

"Yes?"

Here Mr. Fredericks became incoherent again. "It's only that if you were to, you know, do me the honor and so on, it might spur old Bumbershook on a bit, you see."

"*What?*" I demanded, my head whirling.

He regarded me warily. "Now don't get upset again, will you? It's just that if you married into money, especially money on a rather impressive scale, that would be a bit of an inducement for Bumbershook to marry your mother and adopt little Alexander, you see? Not that he needs an inducement, exactly, but it wouldn't occasion quite so much comment in society, if you understand me. And I am not such a bad marriage prospect as a lot of new money is," he added anxiously, "being the grandson of a baron."

I thought about this.

"You're not going to cry, are you? I'd much, *much* rather you were angry."

"So, if I marry you, Mama can marry the man she loves and Alexander will have a future, even a rather exalted future?"

"That's it," he said, nodding.

"And I will have a rich husband?"

"One of the richest in England," he assured me. "And of quite *reasonably* good birth. If I should perform a few services to the crown here and there, you might even find yourself being hailed as 'Lady Fredericks' in a few years."

"But . . . wait! The servants, and the tenants!"

Mr. Fredericks looked bewildered. I explained.

"All my life I have known that the fate of everyone at Crooked Castle depended upon me, and upon my marriage. I cannot abandon them. If Mama marries the Marquis, she and Alexander will leave Yorkshire."

He thought about this. "Yorkshire is going to be a center for industry," he said. "Coal, steel, and textiles. Not here on the coast, perhaps, but in the West Riding. We could buy this property from your brother, rebuild the castle *away* from the cliffs, and keep it as a summer residence, if you like. Would that do?"

"Admirably. And what," I enquired, perhaps hoping for a lover's declaration, "will *you* get out of this arrangement?"

He looked at me, and smiled, a sweet and shy smile. "D'you know? When I first came here, they told me you were one of the most beautiful women in Europe."

I smiled and dropped my gaze to my hands, which were clasped in my lap, waiting.

"Quite frankly?" he said, shaking his head slowly, "I could never see it."

"I *beg* your pardon!"

"I won't be marrying you for your much-vaunted beauty, Miss Crawley." Here he paused and eyed me thoughtfully. "Tho' now I think of it, it may come in handy in the future, at least once we get you some decent clothes."

"*Me!* Get *me* decent clothes?" I stared accusingly at his faded waistcoat and ink-stained jacket.

"Your portrait appearing in the exhibition will help, of course. It will mean my coming out into the open, becoming an 'English gentleman.' And a beautiful wife will help to establish me in society.

"But no, I won't be marrying you for your looks, just as I suspect you won't be marrying me *entirely* for my money."

"As I did not know you had any, sir, you are in the right *there*. And I beg your pardon, but I have not yet said I *would* marry you."

The smile dropped from his face. "Then . . . do you mean you won't?" He looked so desolate that I began to feel quite cheerful.

"You say it is not for my beauty, and it cannot be for my fortune. Once again, therefore, I ask: *why* do you want to marry me?" In truth, I would have married him *whatever* the reason, but still, I wished to understand.

He looked acutely uncomfortable. "Really, I don't know. I suppose it is because I like quarrelling with you. When I went away to London I meant to forget about you, but I couldn't—I found I kept arguing with you in my head. I couldn't concentrate on my work. I made a fool of myself in a meeting with a foundry owner—*you* were there, inside my brain, putting up some utterly ridiculous objection to the terms of the agreement. The man must have thought I was mad.

"In the end I wrote to my mother. She's a clever woman, my mother. She explained that I was so miserable because I was in love with you. And she said I had better get back to Yorkshire before you married Boring. So I thought I would, just to see if she was right."

"And was she?" I asked.

His eyes searched my face. What he saw there seemed to hearten him, because a half-smile formed on his lips. "I expect so; my mother generally *is* right."

I could not help it. I returned his half-smile.

Encouraged, he added, "And *you* like quarrelling with *me* as well, you know you do."

I abruptly covered my face with a hand to hide a laugh.

"Let us agree that we are marrying so we can go on

quarreling in the greatest possible comfort and convenience. Oh, please, Althea, *look* at me. Do say yes."

I relinquished any attempt to control my amusement at this unconventional declaration of devotion, and laughed aloud. "Oh, very well then, yes! I accept. Yes, sir, I will marry you."

An expression like the dawn breaking over the moors transformed his face. "Excellent!" he cried. "Let me have your hand on it," and he proceeded to pump it with great vigor.

"And now that *that* is settled," he said, sounding very cheerful, "what about something to eat? I've the very devil of an appetite."

"So have I," I agreed. "Fido! Come along! It's time to go."

I took Mr. Fredericks's arm and, turning our backs on the ruins of Crooked Castle, we wound our way down the hill towards breakfast, and our little dog ran along behind.

FIN